E.J. GORMAN

Midnight Boundaries (Vol 1)

An Anthology of Tales from Beyond the Veil - Vol. 1

First edition

ISBN (paperback): 979-8-9997840-3-2
ISBN (hardcover): 979-8-9997840-4-9

This book was professionally typeset on Reedsy.
Find out more at reedsy.com

For my wife — Who kept the lights on while I wrote in the dark.

"Whenever you're in a rush, expect delays."

- E.J. GORMAN

Contents

Preface

I didn't set out to write a book.

Like so many others, I found myself searching for a way to cope—to bleed off uncertainty, loneliness, frustration, and despair.

What came out were these strange little worlds.

They arrived uninvited.

One whispered to me from beneath Golgotha's hill, insisting there was more to a sacred story than we had ever been told.

One walked me back through the years of a life well lived—and dared to ask what might happen if we were given the chance to slip behind the curtain and begin again.

One was about a man who craved connection so badly he opened his heart to something he didn't understand.

Written at odd hours of the night, between news cycles and moments of quarantine-induced clarity, these tales became something I clung to. A reminder that even when the world feels unrecognizable, we still have stories—and stories, if we let them, can keep us going.

So I offer you these three. They come from the restless, hopeful part of me that still believes that the unseen matters—that love can be terrifying, that faith can be messy, and that endings are often just doors disguised as conclusions.

Thank you for opening this book.

I hope something inside of it follows you long after you've closed it.

— *E.J. Gorman*

Echoes of Destiny

Most people are already familiar with the tale of Jesus of Nazareth and the events of the last supper—the final meal he shared with his disciples, his betrayal at the hands of Judas Iscariot, and his subsequent arrest in the garden under the cover of night.

They know of his trial before the Sanhedrin, the shouts of blasphemy, and the reluctant Roman governor, Pontius Pilate, who washed his hands of the affair even as he ordered Jesus flogged and crucified. But there's a part of the story you likely haven't heard—a hidden chapter omitted from the ancient scrolls and scriptures. And yet, I assure you friends… it happened.

After that fateful morning, Jesus—beaten, bloodied, and barely conscious— found himself nailed to a rough-hewn wooden cross, flanked by two criminals whose lives were also forfeit. By mid-morning, they were raised up high against the harsh blue sky, a grim tableau for all to see.

For six excruciating hours, Jesus hung in agony, the desert sun baking his skin, every breath a torment. Blood streamed from the wounds on his back, wrists, and feet. His thirst was unbearable. Flies gathered. Crows circled, occasionally swooping to peck at his wounds, seeking an easy meal. Some passersby would mock him, hurling insults, stones, and spit, though the sharpness of his pain dulled even their cruelty. Occasionally, the Roman guards would bark at the rabble to keep their distance if they proved too unruly.

As the sun began its slow descent and shadows lengthened across the hillside, the crowds began to thin. The soldiers nearby busied themselves preparing a crude evening meal, their voices low, their eyes half-lidded from the day's heat. Jesus, meanwhile, slipped in and out of a haze, his vision flickering like the last light of a dying lamp.

Then, from the periphery of his dim awareness, footsteps approached—soft and deliberate. A solitary hooded figure emerged from the fading light, cloaked in shadow. The mysterious figure knelt at the base of the cross, reverent and calm. Jesus felt a hand—gentle & warm—rest upon his foot.

"Rest now, my lord," came a soothing voice from beneath the hood.

He felt a sudden pinch in his foot—not pain, but something else entirely. A warmth surged through him, soothing his pain almost instantly.

Struggling to open his eyes once more, he glimpsed the hooded figure gazing up at him with dark-skinned features and tearful, reverent eyes, one green and the other blue. A white lock of hair dangled near their right eye, while a small silver cross was tattooed beneath their left. "Are you... an ang..." he struggled to ask before coughing from the dryness in his throat, and drawing the attention of the nearby soldiers. "Oi!" shouted one of them upon noticing the hooded figure touching Jesus's foot. "Move away from the criminal now!" His commanding tone allowed no room for argument. The hooded figure glanced in his direction, then turned back to Jesus.

"Who are y..." Jesus began, but the words never came. Darkness overtook him. His head slumped forward, his breath shallowed. After a few moments, to any immediate observer, it would appear as though he'd stopped breathing, his heart no longer beating.

"I said be off with you!" the soldier growled again, this time placing a hand on the hilt of his sword in warning.

The hooded figure, noting the soldier's growing discontent with their presence, nodded and rose slowly, before giving one final glance up at the cross.

"We'll meet again soon," the shadowy figure whispered before turning from Golgotha's hill and disappearing down the winding path toward the city gates of Jerusalem. Wrapped in dusk and shrouded by a crowd returning from the spectacle, the hooded figure easily melted into the throng.

Slipping through narrow alleys and shadowed corners, the figure doubled back through the labyrinthine streets, ensuring that no prying eyes were following. After several turns and passages, the hooded figure came to a door beneath a crooked sign that read: "The Golden Goblet." The image painted beside it depicted a bull dressed as a Roman gladiator, with one horn chopped off, a bull ring through its septum, while hoisting a frothy mug of ale in triumph.

From inside came the familiar din of laughter, breaking glass, and rough voices echoing in the air. The shadowy figure paused, letting out a weary sigh, then reached for the handle and pushed open the door.

* * *

Entering the tavern, the hooded figure paused just inside the threshold, their mismatched eyes scanning the room in a single practiced sweep. The air was thick with smoke, laughter, and the scent of spiced meat and spilled ale. Rowdy patrons filled the space—some engaged in games of fortune, others deep in drunken arguments. In one corner, a group of men who looked to be fighters or gladiators spoke in low, serious tones. Two servant girls moved through the crowd with trays of food and drink, their clothing revealing and their expressions weary, enduring gropes and jeers with a mixture of resignation and defiance.

The mysterious figure's gaze eventually settled on a booth tucked into a far corner, where two men sat, quietly nursing mugs of ale. One was a large man with fair-olive skin, a full beard, and long dark hair that flowed over his shoulders. Beside him sat a smaller man of Middle Eastern descent, his shoulder-length brown hair unkempt, a mustache above his lips and a five-o'clock shadow tracing his jaw.

With measured steps, the figure crossed the tavern floor and slipped into the booth across from them. A quick glance around confirmed that no one nearby was paying them any heed.

The larger man sipped his ale—warm, yet refreshing.

"How'd it go?" he asked once they were alone.

"It's done," the hooded figure replied in a low voice.

Just then, one of the servant girls approached, a crude wooden tray balanced effortlessly in one hand.

"Welcome to the Golden Goblet!" she announced cheerfully to the newcomer. "Can I get you anything?"

The hooded figure remained silent, offering only a small shake of the head.

"We will have another round," the large man said, holding up two fingers to indicate himself and his companion.

"Right away!" the girl replied, turning to leave—only to be slapped on the backside by a drunken patron. She stopped, turned, and smacked the man hard across the face before continuing on her way.

"How long do we have?" the hooded figure asked once the servant girl was out of earshot.

"A little under two days," the smaller man answered before taking a sip of ale.

"Guards?" the larger man inquired.

"Three at the cross." the hooded figure replied evenly.

"Hmm." The larger man grunted thoughtfully as the servant girl returned with their drinks, bringing a quiet pause to the table.

"Here you are!" she said brightly, placing the mugs before them.

"Gratitude," said the larger man as he dropped a silver denarius onto the table. The coin gleamed, bearing the likeness of Emperor Augustus on one side and the image of Pax, the goddess of peace, on the other, and it was worth more than most Romans earned in a day.

As the girl picked up the coin, he added, "Keep it."

Her eyes widened. "Gratitude, m'lord! Enjoy your evening," she said, staring at the generous tip before moving off into the crowd.

"What about Joseph?" the cloaked figure asked once they were alone again.

"He has his instructions," the larger man replied, taking another sip of ale.

"Did you secure rooms?" the mysterious figure asked.

"Yours is upstairs, last door on the left."

"Then I'll retire now and I suggest you both do the same. We have a mission to complete." the hooded figure reminded them.

"We'll be up soon," the larger man replied, raising his mug again as the smaller man followed suit, trying to keep pace.

The shadowy figure gave a slight nod, stood, and ascended the narrow staircase.

Turning right at the top of the landing, the hooded figure followed the dim corridor to the last door on the left. Pushing open the door with a creak, they took in the scene. The room inside was sparse: a single straw bed topped with a rough woolen blanket, a wooden table with a half-burnt candle flickering quietly, and a small window framed by slanted wooden slats, open to the night air.

After closing and latching the door, the hooded figure sat down on the edge of the bed and removed their hood, revealing a young woman in her mid-twenties. Her hair, currently tied in a braid, shimmered like moonlight—a striking contrast to skin the color of ebon ash. Just beneath her left eye was the mark of her order; a silver cross.

Outside, the sun had long since set. Crickets chirped in the brush, their song steady beneath the growing hush of the evening. In the distance, thunder rumbled—a low, brooding growl that rolled across the hills, signaling the approach of a coming storm.

From the streets below, faint voices called out—parents ushering their children indoors as the wind picked up, carrying with it the scent of rain and the last echoes of laughter.

She lay back slowly, staring up at the ceiling. The tension of the day drained from her limbs. That fading laughter clung to her ears like a lullaby—soft, distant, and fleeting.

Sleep found her swiftly. The candle flickered lower.

And the world slipped into darkness.

* * *

Suddenly, she was a little girl again, running barefoot through a sun-dappled field with her sister.

"I'm gonna get you!" she shouted, chasing after her younger twin, Nehir.

"No, you won't!" Nehir called back, her laughter echoing through the open meadow.

"Dilara! Nehir!" Their father's voice rang out across the field, breaking their concentration. "It's almost time for supper!"

"Okay!" they answered in unison, undeterred. They knew they had a few precious minutes left to play before their father's tone went from kind to stern.

The twins, nearly indistinguishable save for their eyes—Nehir with a blue left eye and green right, and Dilara the reverse—giggled as they darted through the tall grass, locked in a spirited game of tag. Nehir, always the quicker of the two, danced just out of reach while Dilara struggled to keep up, panting with exertion.

As she slowed, Dilara watched Nehir vanish into a thicket.

"Nehir!" she called out, recalling their father's strict warnings about straying through the tall grass. "We're not supposed to go in there!"

There was no reply.

Though their appearances mirrored each other, their personalities couldn't have been more different. Nehir was bold, impulsive—always the first to leap, while Dilara was more cautious, hesitant to break the rules.

"Father won't be happy!" she called again, now standing at the edge of the grass, where the stalks towered over her head, thick and impenetrable.

She hesitated, then muttered, "Dammit, Nehir," and pushed her way in.

"Nehir!" she cried again.

"I'm over here!" came the distant voice of her sister.

"Nehir! We're not supposed to go in here!" Dilara protested, forcing her way deeper into the dense undergrowth.

"Come find me!" Nehir's voice giggled from somewhere unseen.

"Nehir! Where are you?" Dilara called, her voice rising with unease.

Then, without warning, a scream tore through the air—high, sharp, and unmistakably Nehir's. It was followed by a chilling silence that froze Dilara in place.

"Nehir?" she whispered. No answer.

"Nehir... this isn't funny..." she murmured, her breath trembling as she pressed forward, her view obscured by the thick wall of grass.

A low growl rumbled from somewhere to her left. Her blood ran cold.

"Nehir?" she said again, inching toward the sound.

The growling deepened, louder now, until she stepped into a small clearing—and froze.

A creature knelt over Nehir's body, devouring her from the waist down. Her lifeless eyes stared blankly at Dilara.

Paralyzed, she stood rooted firmly in place, unable to scream, unable to move.

The creature had mottled reddish skin and webbed wings that twitched with each movement. It hunched over Nehir like a predator savoring its kill.

"Nehir?" Dilara whispered, her voice laced with shock.

The creature, sensing her presence, turned toward her, pausing to chew a morsel of flesh before swallowing it with a guttural sound, its yellowish-red eyes, bulged from its face as it blinked.

Its long, sinewy arms ended in three jagged talons, and from the waist down it bore the legs of a goat, covered in coarse black fur and ending in sharp hooves. Blood slicked its chin and dripped from its claws, painting the grass in crimson.

Their eyes met.

Dilara let out a shriek and the creature howled in response before she jolted upright in bed as a flash of lightning illuminated the room, casting fleeting shadows across the walls, followed by a deep crack of thunder that rolled through the sky like an ancient drum.

She sat up, heart pounding from the dream that'd just released its grip.

Rain tapped steadily against the crooked wooden slats of the inn's window, slipping through the cracks and dripping onto the worn, wooden floorboards. Overhead, a slow, rhythmic leak from the shoddy roof fell into a bucket placed long ago to catch it.

With a quiet breath, she listened as the storm raged outside.

She lay back down and closed her eyes, guessing there were still a few hours until dawn.

This time, her dreams let her be.

* * *

Eventually, the storm abated and the sun crept up behind the clouds, ushering in the day as roosters crowed in a scattered chorus. From below, the scent of spiced stew and fresh bread wafted up to the rooms, stirring Dilara awake. Her stomach growled in protest as she realized she hadn't eaten in nearly a full day.

Rising, she fastened her cloak and checked her belongings. The scent from the kitchen proved too strong to ignore.

Descending the stairs, she entered the inn's dining area, where the servant girl from the night before greeted her cheerfully.

"Good morrow!" she said brightly. A few early patrons sat scattered throughout the room, nibbling on bread, cheese, nuts, and fruit, with mugs of tea or wine in hand.

"Feel free to sit wherever you like."

"Gratitude," Dilara said softly, choosing the same booth as the night before.

Moments later, the servant girl returned. "What can I get you?"

"I will have some of whatever smells so good," Dilara replied, placing a silver denarius on the table.

The servant girl's eyes lit up. "One bowl of lamb stew coming right up!" she chirped, snatching the coin and hurrying toward the kitchen.

Dilara turned her gaze to the window. The street beyond glistened with rain, and her mind drifted—as it often did—to Nehir.

They'd only been twelve when Nehir was taken by the *Erebos Fiend*—named after the Greek god of shadow and darkness. Vile, predatory creatures that thrived in the shadows, possessed of unnatural speed and a taste for human flesh. Even now, the memory twisted her gut.

"Morning," greeted Magnus, the leader of the trio. His gravelly voice pulling Dilara from her thoughts as he slid into the seat across from her, looking just as he had the night before—calm, unreadable.

"Good morning," she echoed.

The servant girl returned with a steaming bowl of stew and a roughly carved wooden spoon.

"Here you go," she said, placing it down with a smile.

Dilara took the spoon, dipped it in, and took a bite, immediately wincing as the scalding broth singed her tongue.

"And what can I get you, m'lord?" the servant girl asked, turning toward Magnus.

"I will have the same," he replied with a nod toward Dilara's bowl.

"And an ale," he added, tossing the servant girl a wink.

"Coming right up, m'lord!" she replied, smiling.

"Isn't it a bit early for ale?" Dilara asked once the servant the girl had left.

Magnus merely shrugged. "It's five o'clock somewhere." he answered, peering through the nearby window.

Dilara rolled her eyes and blew on another spoonful of stew.

"How is it?" he asked.

"It's really good," she replied, cautiously taking another bite, savoring the flavor.

"Where's Lucian?" she asked between bites.

"Probably sleeping off last night's drink," Magnus replied. "Lightweight Lucian—living up to the name."

Dilara smirked. Her mind flashed back to when she'd first met Lucian. They'd played a drinking game to test their endurance. Three strong drinks in, and Lucian had lost his lunch across the floor—earning him a nickname he'd never escape.

She chuckled softly, savoring another bite of her stew.

"We should probably wake him," she suggested.

"Soon enough," Magnus said, settling back. "We've got a little time to kill."

The servant girl reappeared with a second steaming bowl and a large tankard of ale.

"Here you go!" she said cheerfully, setting them down in front of Magnus.

"Gratitude," he replied, tossing her another silver denarius.

"Oh, you are *so* very welcome, m'lord! Enjoy!" she beamed, tucking the coin away and heading off.

Magnus wasted no time. He dove into his stew, steam rising as he tore through it, barely noticing the heat. Dilara watched in awe as he finished it all in under a minute, lifted the bowl, and drank the broth straight down.

"Did you even taste it?" she asked as he set the bowl down and burped lightly.

"Yeah. And you're right, it was good," he said, lifting his tankard and draining a long swig.

Footsteps creaked from the stairs.

"Morning," came Lucian's hoarse voice as he stumbled toward their booth. His hair was wild, his eyes bleary, and the smell of ale still clung to him like a second cloak.

Dilara slid over to make room as he joined them, groaning.

"I'm never drinking again," he muttered, eyeing her half-eaten bowl of stew. A sudden rumble in his stomach made him freeze.

"Oh no..." he groaned.

Without warning, he shot up, bolted past the servant girl, and disappeared through the exit.

Dilara and Magnus turned toward the window just in time to see him stagger into the middle of the street and vomit violently, causing a few passersby to recoil in disgust.

"Uhu, heard that before," Magnus muttered, smirking.

Dilara shook her head and returned to her stew. Magnus watched, amused, as Lucian stumbled to a nearby water trough, where a donkey was already drinking. As Lucian approached, it sidestepped, snorting in protest.

Lucian paid it no heed, instead plunging his head straight into the water.

The donkey squealed, startled, but soon realized that Lucian posed no real threat and returned to drinking beside him as though nothing were amiss.

Suppressing laughter and shaking his head, Magnus turned back to Dilara.

"We're heading out soon," he said between sips. "Need to pay a visit to Joseph." He said as he watched Lucian, who'd resurfaced and dunked himself again with grim determination.

"Ready when you are," Dilara replied, finishing the last of her stew.

"Now's as good a time as any, I guess," Magnus said, draining the rest of his ale in a single gulp. He belched softly, wiped his mouth, and stood before heading for the door.

Dilara rose and followed.

"Have a pleasant day!" the servant girl called after them as they stepped out of the tavern.

Lucian, still dripping but noticeably more coherent, looked up as they approached.

"You gonna be all right?" Magnus asked as they passed the trough.

"I'll be fine," Lucian grunted, running a hand through his soaked hair.

"We've got a bit of a walk ahead," Magnus called over his shoulder as he and Dilara strode into the street.

"Right behind you, boss," Lucian muttered, falling into step as the three disappeared into the waking city.

* * *

Soon, they were on the road, heading northwest toward the city of Arimathea. The bustling thoroughfare was alive with activity. Horse-drawn carriages creaked along the stone path, and donkeys laden with silks, furs, and fragrant spices carried wealthy nobles draped in fine garments.

By mid-afternoon, they'd arrived at their destination: a grand house nestled at the edge of the city. Its high stone walls were topped with a gently sloping tiled roof that cast shade over a wide, carefully maintained courtyard. As they approached the main entrance, Dilara couldn't help but marvel at the craftsmanship of the door—solid oak, carved with intricate scenes and symbols of prosperity. Polished brass fittings caught the sunlight and gleamed, a testament to years of care and wealth.

Magnus cast a quick glance over his shoulder to ensure they weren't being followed, then knocked three times, paused, then a fourth.

Moments later, the door swung opened, revealing a tall, dignified figure.

Joseph of Arimathea stood framed in the doorway. His silver hair and well-kept beard lent him an air of quiet authority. He wore a finely woven robe of deep blue, decorated with subtle patterns of vines and waves, and his eyes, though kind, held the weight of wisdom.

"Welcome, friends," he greeted warmly, extending a weathered hand. "Please, do come in."

As the trio entered, Joseph cast a final glance over the street before closing the door behind them and sliding a thick wooden latch into place.

"Welcome, welcome," he repeated, guiding them into a spacious and beautifully appointed living area. Sturdy wooden tables bore carvings of pastoral scenes—shepherds, sheep, olive groves—while cushioned benches and chairs in rich fabrics lined the walls. A large, colorful rug covered the stone floor beneath their feet, its geometric designs still vibrant with age. Tapestries depicting ancient myths adorned the walls, and in one corner, a bronze oil lamp flickered gently, casting a warm amber glow. Shelves displayed clay pottery, woven baskets, and other carefully arranged pieces—each one a testament to Joseph's appreciation for art and craftsmanship.

The trio settled onto a broad bench meant for communal seating.

"Would any of you care for some tea?" Joseph offered.

"No," said Magnus flatly.

"No, thank you," Dilara added with a polite shake of her head.

"I will have some," Lucian piped up, already perking up at the thought.

"Right away!" Joseph said cheerfully, disappearing into the adjoining kitchen.

"He seems nice," Lucian said casually once they were alone.

Moments later, Joseph returned with a clay teacup, its surface painted with delicate floral patterns and the handle shaped with elegant curves. He handed it to Lucian, who accepted it with cautious delight, taking a tentative sip as Magnus watched him with a raised brow.

Joseph then took a seat opposite them in a wooden chair padded with cushions.

"What news?" Magnus asked once everyone had settled.

"Well, I was able to meet with Governor Pilate," Joseph replied, his tone calm but deliberate. "And after offering a significant sum of coin, I was granted custody of our lord's remains and have placed them in my own tomb, as we discussed."

Magnus nodded approvingly.

"And per your instructions," Joseph continued, "we stocked the tomb with food and water to sustain him after he has... arisen." Joseph said with a hint of uncertainty.

"Very good," said Magnus. "Any complications?"

Joseph hesitated.

"Yes, I am afraid there is a problem. The Sanhedrin council has caught wind of the prophecy of our lord's return. As such, they've stationed guards at the tomb to ensure nothing... miraculous occurs."

"How many?" Dilara asked.

"Three, by my count." Joseph replied.

As he listened, Magnus's gaze drifted to a painting on the wall—angels and demons locked in battle, their wings distinguishing them: some white, some black. Lightning crackled in the scene, and the weapons they wielded radiated divine energy. The chaotic beauty of the image stirred something in him. The memories of his own battles flickered in his mind: the clash of shadows, the stench of sulfur, the screams of the dying.

"We can handle the guards," Lucian said, interrupting the silence as he sipped his tea.

"Excellent!" Joseph quipped. "Then I shall leave the rest in your capable hands," he added firmly. "Do you require anything else of me?"

"No," Magnus replied. "You have done well." he added, eliciting a nod from Joseph.

"We move tonight." Magnus said as he looked to his companions, who both nodded in agreement.

"In that case, please, make yourselves at home," Joseph offered, standing. "I have other matters to attend to, but if you need anything at all, please do not hesitate to call on me."

He turned and disappeared into another room.

Magnus rose and stretched, glancing around before finding a spot near the fire on a luxurious rug. He lay down, resting his head on his folded arms.

"Get some rest, you two," he said. "It's going to be an early morning."

Dilara eased into the cushioned bench, adjusting her cloak as she settled in. Lucian joined Magnus on the rug and lay back with a sigh.

Before long, they were both snoring soundly.

Dilara lingered a while longer, her thoughts once again turning to Nehir —her laughter, her daring nature, her screams of agony. Soon, Dilara's eyes were too heavy to keep open and she too drifted off to sleep.

* * *

There she was again—a little girl, standing in the tall grass, face-to-face with the Erebos fiend as it swallowed a chuck of flesh torn from her sister's lifeless body. She screamed and turned to flee, the monster shrieking as it gave chase.

Dilara sprinted as fast as her legs would carry her, the sound of the fiend closing in behind her. From beyond the tall grass, her father's voice echoed: "Dilara! Nehir! Where are you?!"

"Father…!" she tried to answer, but the creature tackled her from behind, slamming her into the earth with a triumphant screech. It pinned her down, and leaned in, its reeking breath washing over her face, making her gag.

Her father's voice rang out again—desperate, searching.

The fiend paused, raising its head, its milky-yellowish eyes turning toward the sound. Then, it looked down at its prey, before raising its talon to strike.

Without warning, the ground began to rumble, causing the creature to falter. The beast snarled in confusion—before it was suddenly wrenched from on top of her and hurled backward.

"Dilara! To me! Now!" her father's voice boomed.

She scrambled to her feet and turned toward the sound. There stood her father, one hand pressed to his temple, the other outstretched toward the creature, suspended in mid-air as if held by invisible chains. It shrieked and writhed, unable to break free. Her father's face was tight with focus.

"Get behind me! Now!" he commanded.

She obeyed, rushing to his side.

The fiend thrashed, frothing with rage, but her father didn't flinch.

"Die, foul fiend!" he growled, slowly curling his outstretched hand into a fist.

The air rippled. The creature's limbs snapped inward with grotesque crunches. Black ichor gushed from its contorted body as it howled in pain. With a final squeeze, her father crushed the beast into a pulsing mass of gore, some of it splattering across his face and clothes. Finally, he released his hold, and the mangled corpse of the creature dropped to the ground, still twitching.

Silence fell.

"Father," Dilara whispered, barely able to speak.

He turned to her, kneeling gently. The fury in his eyes melting into concern. "My dearest Dilara... where is Nehir?" He held her shoulders, voice trembling. He gave her a shake. "Where is your sister?"

Dilara opened her mouth, but no words came. Her memory surged—the monster, the tearing, Nehir's screams—all she could do was point in the direction of Nehir's body.

Her father rose and followed her gesture. A moment later, his agonized cries echoed through the field as he cradled Nehir's lifeless body in his arms.

Dilara, blinking and dazed, approached the remains of the creature—her grief curdling into rage.

Without a word, she attacked—stomping it with her foot—until she was soaked in its blood and viscera. Only when her fury broke did she stagger to her father's side and collapse beside him, sobbing uncontrollably.

Nehir's head rested against their father's shoulder, her vacant eyes still fixed on Dilara.

Then she spoke.

"It's time," Nehir said softly.

Dilara's breath caught. Her father held the body, his own tears still falling in silence.

"Time for what?" she whispered, dazed.

"Time to wake up," came Magnus's familiar voice, piercing the dream and snapping Dilara back to consciousness.

Lucian was already sitting up.

"Feeling better?" she asked, rising with a groggy breath.

"Yeah," Lucian nodded. "I needed that."

He stood, stretching as he glanced around. "Joseph?" he inquired.

"Asleep upstairs," Magnus replied. "He's going to miss all the fun," Lucian said with a smirk.

"He left supplies for the journey," Magnus added, gesturing to a brown satchel brimming with fruits and nuts beside a water filled skin.

"That was nice of him," Lucian remarked, cracking open a nut and popping it into his mouth.

"Let's go. Grab the supplies, Lucian," Magnus urged.

They each donned their hooded cloaks. Lucian collected the provisions, and the three quietly made their way to the entrance of Joseph's home.

"We need to stay out of sight," Magnus reminded them as he opened the door. The crescent moon hung high overhead, bathing the world in pale silver light.

He stepped out first, followed by Lucian and Dilara who closed the door behind her.

Soon, the trio had disappeared into the night.

They followed the road south, heading back toward Jerusalem under the cloak of darkness. Before long, they approached their destination: the tomb of Joseph's family.

"It should be just over that hill," Lucian said, pointing toward a rise where the road split.

"Off the road, now," Magnus commanded.

They slipped into the woods and crept in the direction of the tomb. When they reached the tree line, they crouched, eyes fixed on the site before them.

Joseph's family tomb stood solemnly beneath the moonlight. A heavy, circular stone slab sealed the entrance, its surface weathered and etched with ancient markings. Three Roman soldiers sat nearby, huddled around a fire, passing a water skin and murmuring quietly.

"Three guards, just like he said," Lucian whispered.

"What's the plan?" Dilara asked.

"We scare them off," Magnus said calmly.

"How?" she asked.

"We shake things up," he replied with a wink.

Dilara gave a nod. "Understood."

"You know what to do," Magnus told Lucian.

"Indeed I do, boss," Lucian said with a grin, breaking off from the group and slipping silently around toward the back of the tomb.

Within moments, Lucian signaled his readiness. "He's in position." Magnus confirmed.

"Ready when you are," he nodded toward Dilara, giving her the cue.

She stood and lowered her hood. Her white hair shimmered faintly in the moonlight. Raising her right hand toward the tomb, she placed her left against her temple and closed her eyes.

The sounds of the forest grew quiet and time itself seemed to halt.

Dilara summoned the image—her sister's death, the beast, the pain—and let the rage sharpen her focus. In her mind, she let out a primal scream as her eyes snapped open and glowed like holy flame.

The ground suddenly trembled beneath them, so violently that Magnus nearly lost his footing, forcing him to grab a nearby tree to steady himself.

"The earth!" one of the soldiers cried, standing up and drawing his sword. "It quakes!"

"What is happening?!" another shouted.

Dilara remained steadfast, holding out her hand as she channeled raw energy like a conduit in the direction of the tomb. The stone slab sealing the tomb began to roll—slowly at first, then with undeniable force.

"The tomb! It opens!" another soldier shouted.

The slab rolled aside with a low rumble. The ground suddenly pitched, toppling the soldiers to their knees. When the entrance was fully revealed, Dilara lowered her hand and the trembling stopped as quickly as it had begun.

The guards scrambled to their feet on high alert, swords drawn, their eyes wide with fear.

"What sorcery is this?!" shouted one of the guards as he scanned the perimeter, looking for whoever was responsible for the disturbance.

17

"Greetings!" came a cheerful voice from above, drawing the attention of the soldiers.

Lucian sat atop the tomb's archway, legs casually dangling, now appearing as an angel in flowing white robes, glowing with an ethereal light. Large wings flapped behind him, folding neatly behind his back.

"Do you have a moment to talk about our Lord and savior?" he asked with a friendly wave.

The soldiers froze, their eyes widened in shock—then they collapsed in a heap, unconscious.

"Well, that was easy," Lucian chuckled, hopping down and snapping his fingers to dispel the illusion. "All clear!"

Magnus and Dilara emerged from the trees and joined him.

"Are they okay?" Dilara asked.

"They'll live, I think," Lucian replied with a shrug.

"Let's do what we came to do," Magnus said, heading toward the tomb entrance.

"I'll go in," Dilara offered. "He's seen my face."

Magnus studied her for a moment, then nodded. "Alright. Be quick. Others may be coming."

She slipped into the darkness of the tomb. The only light came from the moon outside and the dying fire behind her.

"Who is there?" a voice called from deeper inside.

"I was there... at the cross," she answered softly.

A figure stirred from the darkness and leaned forward into the light. Jesus was wrapped in burial cloth, still stained with dried blood. His eyes fixed on her.

"It is you," he said, his voice laced with awe. "I thought I was dreaming."

"You were not dreaming," she replied.

"Am I dead?" he asked, his voice trembling.

"No, my lord," she whispered. "You are not dead. Far from it."

He looked down at the wounds on his wrists and feet, now healed as if they'd never been there at all.

"How is this possible?" he asked.

"All will be explained," she said gently, placing a hand on his arm.

Their eyes met and for a moment, she felt him looking straight through her—into her soul.

"I believe you," he murmured.

Lucian's voice called from outside. "Hey, we need to hurry."

"Okay," she answered, then turned back to Jesus, her voice softening. "Can you walk?"

"I think so," he said, rising unsteadily. He stumbled, then steadied himself with her help. "Yes, I can walk."

Together, they stepped out into the night.

"Let's move," Magnus commanded, already leading the way back into the woods, with Lucian, Dilara, and Jesus following closely behind.

Behind them, the sound of approaching guards echoed down the road—but by the time they'd arrived, the group was already well away and the tomb itself sat empty.

The three fainted guards could offer only one word, repeated through chattering teeth:

"Angel."

* * *

The quartet moved quickly through the woods. Somewhere behind them, the distant barking of dogs echoed—faint but persistent. After a while, the noise faded into nothingness.

"May we rest soon?" Jesus asked.

"Soon," Magnus replied, his voice steady.

Silence followed until Jesus spoke again. "Where are we going, friends?"

"To a safe place." Magnus replied, offering no further detail.

Jesus accepted the answer with a nod. "Very well."

After a moment, he looked around and asked plainly, "So, who are you people?"

The group halted.

Magnus turned and approached him. Jesus instinctively stepped back, but

Magnus placed a calm hand upon his shoulder.

"My Lord," he said, "all will be explained in due time."

His voice softened, and he allowed a rare, uncertain smile to cross his face.

Jesus regarded him, then nodded slowly. "I understand."

Magnus gave a satisfied nod and continued walking, the others following.

But without warning, Jesus turned and sprinted away into the woods.

Magnus stopped and exhaled. "We don't have time for this."

"I've got him," Dilara said, already running.

Jesus stumbled, still unaccustomed to his restored strength. Dilara caught up quickly and reached out, placing a gentle hand on his arm.

"Wait," she said softly.

"Release me!" he shouted, attempting to pull free.

"It is going to be all right," she said gently, her calm voice breaking through the panic.

He stopped. His eyes met hers. Something in her gaze quieted the storm within him.

"We are taking you to safety. That is all we can say right now. But you must trust us."

Jesus held her gaze. "Very well," he said, breathing easier. "I trust you."

Soon, they returned to the others.

"Let us keep moving," Magnus said.

They walked for what felt like hours, until finally they stepped out into a moonlit clearing.

"How much time do we have?" Magnus asked.

Lucian studied the sky. "An hour—maybe less."

"Then we rest here," Magnus decided, lowering himself onto a log.

Jesus sat cross-legged nearby. "What will happen in an hour?"

Lucian gave a wide smile. "You will see."

Jesus tilted his head. "I am not sure I like the sound of that."

He lowered himself to the ground and looked skyward.

Dilara sat beside him, leaning back on her hands.

"Do not worry," she said. "It is better for you to see it for yourself than it is for us to try to explain it."

Jesus turned his head to look at her. "See what?"

She lay back beside him. "The miracle."

Just then, a shooting star traced a line of light across the sky.

Jesus watched it disappear, then turned to Dilara and asked calmly, "Are you angels?"

Dilara smiled softly. "No, my Lord… we are not angels."

"Did God send you?" he asked after a moment.

"In a way," she answered, her tone guarded.

He rolled onto his side to face her. "Then you do serve God?"

Dilara's gaze grew distant. Her thoughts slipped to a memory long buried.

She was fifteen. The Lord Master had called her before the altar, a grizzled man in his sixties with a red cross on his robe and a silver one tattooed beneath his left eye. He'd seen her potential—her gift, passed from her father: the ability to move matter with her mind.

"Do you swear to serve Almighty God in this life and beyond?" he'd asked, his blade resting lightly upon her shoulder.

"I do, my Lord," she'd answered without hesitation.

"Then I dub thee, Dame Knight!" he'd proclaimed, and her brethren had cheered.

The memory faded. She returned to the present and met Jesus's eyes.

"I do," she said softly.

A single tear rolled down her cheek.

Jesus reached out and brushed it away with his thumb. "What burdens you?"

She stared into the sky. "These are not tears of sorrow, my Lord," she said. "Only memory."

A wolf's howl echoed faintly in the distance.

Jesus regarded her quietly, his gaze lingering longer than he'd intended.

She turned, meeting his eyes. "What?"

Flustered, he looked away. "Forgive me," he said softly. "I… I did not mean to stare."

She smiled quietly, but said nothing.

"I simply cannot wait to see this miracle you spoke of," he added, placing his hands behind his head. "You know, I have performed a few miracles of my own," he said casually.

"So, I have heard," she replied with a knowing grin.

They fell into a comfortable silence, watching the stars wheel across the heavens.

After some time, the wind shifted.

A sudden gust swept through the clearing, and thunder growled on the horizon.

Lucian moved quickly, preparing their supplies.

Jesus sat up, watching the lightning flash in the distance. "What is happening? Is God angry?"

"No," Dilara said, placing a steady hand on his arm. "This is not his wrath."

Without warning, lightning struck a nearby tree, shattering it with a deafening crack. Flames leapt from the splintered bark.

The earth beneath them trembled. A strange, low groan filled the air—as if the very ground were being torn asunder.

"What is happening!?" Jesus shouted over the rising chaos.

"The miracle! It's coming!" Dilara replied, gripping his arm to steady him.

Then came a sound like the ripping of fabric and suddenly, a portal split the air.

It pulsed with red, crackling energy and shimmered with a yellow-green haze. Shaped like a rough, jagged diamond, it grew wide enough for a person to pass through.

"Let's go!" Magnus shouted, stepping boldly into the light.

Jesus watched, stunned, as Magnus vanished through the rippling portal.

"What magic is this?" he asked in awe.

"All will be explained," Dilara urged. "You have nothing to fear."

Lucian turned with a grin, "See you on the other side!" he quipped before giving a mock salute, and stepping through the portal.

Jesus hesitated. "Is this a doorway to another world?"

"It is a place where you are needed, my Lord," she said gently.

He turned toward her, curious.

Her mismatched eyes held him. He'd never seen their like before. He made a quiet promise to ask her about them later.

"Then let us go," he said with renewed determination, offering her his arm.

She took it, and together they stepped into the light.

A wave of warmth passed over them—and when it faded, they found themselves in a chamber of radiant white, surrounded by pristine walls that shimmered with light.

The portal sealed behind them with a gentle *whum*, its edges vanishing without a trace.

Jesus stood on a raised platform, his gaze sweeping the space around him. They were in a vast, luminous chamber—its floor gleaming like marble, its walls lined with braziers burning clean, blue flames.

Surrounding them were scores of men clad in brilliant white robes, each one adorned with a crimson cross upon their chest and a silver cross tattooed beneath their left eye. Their expressions bore discipline and reverence.

As one, they dropped to a single knee.

Jesus turned, startled to see Dilara, Lucian, and Magnus also kneeling, heads bowed in his direction.

"What is this?" Jesus asked, eyes scanning the scene before settling on Dilara, confusion in his voice.

Before she could answer, a deep, commanding voice echoed from behind the crowd.

"My Lord!"

Jesus turned.

A figure emerged—a tall man garbed in black, robes stitched with red threads in the same cross motif. At his hip, he bore a sheathed sword. His face was marked by time and wisdom, and the same silver cross lay beneath his eye.

The man stepped forward, then drew his blade with reverent precision. The steel rang out like a chime through the chamber.

Jesus instinctively tensed.

"Welcome," the man declared, voice rich and solemn, "to the Order of the Knights Templar!

He dropped to one knee and raised his sword to Jesus—a gesture of ancient loyalty and sacred fealty.

Jesus stepped forward slowly and accepted the weapon. The hilt was warm to the touch.

He turned the blade in his hands, eyes catching the intricate runes etched into the steel—symbols foreign to him, yet strangely familiar. The metal shimmered, polished to a mirror-like finish, and in its surface he saw his own reflection.

"Our Lord has returned!" the Lord Master proclaimed, rising to his feet.

A thunderous cheer erupted from the assembly.

Still dazed, Jesus turned to Dilara.

"What is happening? Where are we now?" he asked.

"You are in the future, my Lord," she said gently, rising to her feet.

"Two thousand one hundred and twenty five years beyond your time, my lord." The Lord Master declared loudly.

"Two thousand years…" Jesus whispered, eyes wide with astonishment as he turned again to take in the chamber, the people, and the sheer impossibility of it all.

The Lord Master stood beside him, beaming with reverence.

Across the chamber, the warriors raised their fists in unison.

"Hail!" they cried. "Hail to the Returned One!"

Their voices thundered through the chamber, eyes alight with hope—for they knew now without a shadow of a doubt, that the tide of the demon invasion would soon turn in their favor. But hope, as history has often shown, is a fragile thing—shaped as much by belief as by the truths that lie beneath it.

TBC

Life

Adam Cabrera was a man in his late nineties, his body now frail and tethered to the quiet hum of life support in a sterile hospital room. Around him gathered his family—his children, their spouses, and a scattering of grandchildren—all drawn together in a quiet vigil of remembrance and farewell.

He'd been born to a Scottish father and an Irish mother, a spirited union that gave Adam a stubborn streak and a sharp wit.

Like most people, much of his early childhood was a haze, moments half-remembered and filled in by the photo albums his mother had so meticulously assembled over the years. She'd documented everything. Every laugh, scrape, birthday, and milestone was preserved in glossy pages with handwritten captions.

There was a photo from his first birthday party—held in a quaint English town where his father, then an aircraft mechanic, had been stationed. The black-and-white image showed a yard full of unfamiliar children with paper hats, surrounding a cake crowned by an edible clown. One snapshot captured Adam gleefully smashing the clown-faced confection with both fists, icing smeared across his cheeks.

His father, a gruff but occasionally humorous man, would often recount a particularly embarrassing episode that became something of a family legend. One afternoon, while browsing a local record store, he'd lost track of his toddler son as he sifted through vinyl records. A sudden, unmistakable odor caught his attention.

Looking down, he found little Adam had both urinated and defecated on the store's linoleum floor. Mortified, his father scooped him up and bolted out the door, leaving the unfortunate cleanup to some bewildered clerk. Years later, they would laugh about the incident over beers—memories softened by time and the buffer of fatherhood.

Despite such stories, Adam and his father were never particularly close. The divorce had seen his father retreat overseas, a calculated move to dodge child support obligations. He would remarry several times, always to women considerably younger, women who, to most observers, seemed more interested in his dwindling bank account than in the man himself.

* * *

After the separation, Adam's mother moved him and his baby brother Johnny to Florida—a place they'd once visited together as a family before things fell apart. It was a sun-soaked sanctuary she'd fallen in love with, and she was determined to start fresh there, raising her sons beneath swaying palms and warm southern skies.

As Adam lay in his hospital bed, the soft, rhythmic beeping of the life support machines echoing like a fading heartbeat, his mind drifted back through the years. One of the earliest memories that surfaced from his new life in Florida was a jarring one.

He'd been just a boy when he and his family strolled down to the beach one afternoon, the salty air and sound of crashing waves giving the illusion of peace. But that tranquility was shattered when they stumbled upon a group of local fishermen. They'd hauled in a shark—some species Adam couldn't identify—and were brutally, and illegally, decapitating it right there on the sand.

The shark thrashed weakly as its head was severed, crimson water soaking the shore, while horrified tourists and children looked on in stunned silence. That image—visceral, wrong, unforgettable—burned itself into Adam's young mind. It would never leave him.

* * *

As the years passed, Adam began to learn that the threatening phone calls from his estranged father—usually prompted by his mother's frustration—were just noise. Bark without bite. His father's fury had no teeth across the ocean. That realization gave Adam a sense of freedom. Maybe too much of it.

He fell in with a rougher crowd. Local kids, some from broken homes, others just bored and wild. One of them was a wiry, fast-talking kid named Tony, who had a knack for getting into trouble and a magnetic sort of confidence that drew others in.

Tony once convinced Adam that smoking banana leaves would get them high. This was after they'd already been stealing packs of cigarettes from a local K-Mart and stuffing them into their socks before sprinting out of the automatic doors, like it was a game. It wasn't long before Tony got his hands on what he called "the real stuff," courtesy of his older brother Jack. They'd pack it into a small, dented metal pipe and pass it back and forth, coughing and laughing.

* * *

Adam remembered one time in particular: It was the day of a video game contest at the local Blockbuster—a Street Fighter tournament or something like it. Stoned and hazy, he still managed to land in the top three. He remembered the weird pride he felt, smiling like he'd just won gold in the Olympics. But that feeling was short-lived.

A darker memory followed—the first time Tony pressured him into drinking. It was a warm evening, the cicadas buzzing in the trees, and Tony handed Adam a forty-ounce bottle of malt liquor. The stench hit him first—acrid, bitter, like something gone sour. Adam had tried beer before; occasionally during his childhood, his father would offer him a sip, and each time, he'd spat it out and declared it "gross." This was worse.

But Tony, bigger and broader, wasn't asking. He was demanding. His tone shifted, suddenly sharp and threatening. "Drink it," he'd said, his voice low. "Or I swear I'll knock your teeth out and make sure everyone at school knows what a little pussy you are."

Adam's hands trembled as he raised the bottle, swallowing mouthful after mouthful of the vile liquid until the bottle clinked empty on the sidewalk. He wiped his mouth, let out a burp, and blinked—there were two Tonys now.

"Whoa... I think I'm drunk," Adam slurred.

Tony laughed, clapped him on the back, and said, "Let's go for a walk."

They wandered the sleepy suburban streets, the sky now a deep navy blanket dotted with stars. Streetlights buzzed overhead, casting long shadows on the pavement. Eventually, they made their way to a nearby gas station and ran into another group of teens—this one led by Tyler, one of the school's notorious bullies.

Tyler had made a habit of mocking Adam in the past, calling him "nerd," "teacher's pet," or worse. But tonight was different. Whether it was the malt liquor or something deeper stirring inside, Adam didn't flinch.

When Tyler stepped forward and tried to mouth off, Adam squared his shoulders and snapped back, the sharpness of his words cutting cleaner than he expected. Tyler blinked, hesitated, then backed off.

He never bothered Adam again.

* * *

As the memory faded, Adam's lips curled into a faint, bittersweet smile. Even now, at the edge of consciousness, he could still taste the rebellion of youth— the sting, the triumph, the foolishness, the courage. It'd all blended into the strange, wild mosaic of his life.

Adam Cabrera had made his peace. The decision to remove life support had been his—quiet, resolute, and without fear. Now, surrounded by family in a softly lit hospital room, he lay with machines murmuring gently at his side, each breath mechanical, each beep a fading metronome.

His son William and daughter Tracy stood close, gripping his hands tightly, their hearts aching. Tears shimmered in their eyes as they prepared to say goodbye, not only to their father but to a chapter of their lives. Just a week earlier, their beloved mother Lucy had passed peacefully in her sleep. And now, they found a bittersweet comfort in knowing he'd soon be reunited with her.

As their warm hands pressed into his fragile ones, Adam's thoughts began to drift—memories bubbling up from the deep well of time. One surfaced with unusual clarity.

* * *

It was a warm summer night, in 1992 , when he'd first laid eyes on Lucy. She stood in line ahead of him at the local arcade, waiting for a turn at the latest video game marvel.

Adam had no idea what the game entailed. All he knew in that moment was that the girl standing in front of him, with short, shoulder-length dark hair and piercing brown eyes, had stolen his breath. She was beautiful—effortlessly so. Every line, every glance, every movement seemed to belong to a different world.

But, being the shy young man he was, he didn't have the guts to speak to her.

Instead, he watched as she climbed into her seat, where a worker gently lowered a sleek, glowing headset over her head. The arcade was a riot of LED lights and chiming machines, but somehow, she was the only thing he could see.

Her chair slid back and locked into place. Then it was his turn.

A staff member gestured toward the seat next to hers, and Adam practically leapt in. "Get ready for the ride of your life, kid," the attendant said with a grin as he secured the headset over Adam's eyes.

Suddenly, silence. The noise of the arcade vanished replaced by soft music from his headphones. As the image in his vision took shape, he saw that he was seated in what looked like the front car of a roller coaster, the tracks vanishing into the digital horizon. He turned his head in wonder.

"This is crazy! It looks so real!" he marveled before a voice echoed all around him. *"Welcome. Please sit back and enjoy the ride."*

And then, it began.

The coaster climbed and dropped, twisted and spun. The wind felt real, the momentum dizzying. Then, without warning, the scenery melted into a vortex of shifting colors—a tunnel of pulsating light and sound.

A few moments later, the words **RIDE OVER** flashed in his field of vision, and everything went dark.

"That's it?" he muttered in disbelief as his seat slid forward and another worker helped remove his headset.

"That was… disappointing," he said aloud, stepping off the platform. But then, he spotted her—Lucy—now standing alone at an arcade cabinet, her fingers deftly hammering buttons.

He hesitated for only a second, then walked over to her.

"Mind if I join you?" he asked.

She glanced at him, then gave a small nod. He popped in a quarter and took the joystick beside her. They started playing, exchanging glances and shy smiles, small talk turning into laughter. It turned out they shared more than a love for vintage video games.

From that moment, something unspoken had begun. And soon, they were inseparable.

* * *

His memories shifted to their wedding a few years later in a humble courthouse ceremony. At the time, Adam was working a low-paying job while renting a room from a shrill old landlady who seemed to blame him for every creak in the floorboards. Money was tight, and a grand wedding was out of reach. But as he slid the ring onto Lucy's finger, he whispered, "Someday, baby," a promise wrapped in hope.

Not even a year later, Lucy gave birth to William. And shortly after that came Tracy—his "Irish twin." Together, they built a life from the ground up, juggling work and family, dreams and deadlines.

But time, as it always does, raced forward.

Before he could blink, their children were fully grown, graduates, professionals, parents themselves. The house grew quieter, the rooms filled more often with echoes than with voices.

Now, as he lay on his final bed, a tiny hand was placed gently in his. His great-granddaughter Ellie—barely two years old—stared up at him with large almond-brown eyes full of innocence and wonder. Her gaze locked with his, soft and unblinking.

A single tear slipped down Adam's cheek.

It wasn't from sadness, but from the quiet joy of knowing: he'd lived, truly lived—and the story he and Lucy wrote together would carry on in the eyes of the next generation.

* * *

"It's time," the doctor said softly as he stepped into the room, his nurse close behind.

Adam's family instinctively moved aside as the nurse began the final preparations. One by one, the machines that were sustaining him began to fall silent. The soft hum of oxygen faded. The mechanical rhythm of the ventilator slowed and stopped. Only the heart monitor remained, its beeping growing more sporadic as Adam's heartbeat began its final descent.

"He has a few minutes," the doctor whispered gently to William, whose composure crumbled beneath a fresh wave of tears.

"We'll give you some privacy," the doctor added, nodding to his nurse before the two quietly exited the room.

The family gathered in close now, forming a protective circle around Adam. He could feel their warmth, and their love, in that final moment. His chest rose and fell with effort, each breath shallower than the last. He reached for the hands of his children—one in each hand—and squeezed with what little strength he had left.

"I love you all," he murmured, voice barely audible.

"We love you too, Dad," William and Tracy whispered back, their tears falling freely now, cascading down their cheeks as they held his hands tightly.

Adam's vision blurred. The room began to dim. The last image he saw was the faces of his family, crowded around him—faces full of love, sorrow, and gratitude.

Then, darkness… Complete, resolute darkness.

He felt a sudden sense of dread when suddenly, a light came.

At first it was soft, like the rising sun on a misty morning. Then it grew—brighter, wider, and impossibly radiant. He felt himself being pulled toward it, his body light as air, as if he were no longer bound to flesh and bone. The sensation was peaceful. Uplifting. He didn't know where he was going, but somehow, he knew he belonged there.

Faster and faster he drifted toward the brilliance, which seemed both far away and right in front of him. His surroundings faded into whiteness—pure, blinding white.

And then… darkness again.

Just for a moment at least.

Then came the words; Words he recalled seeing once in his youth.

RIDE OVER

They flashed across his vision in bold, blocky letters, and suddenly, the darkness peeled away.

Adam blinked.

The sounds of beeping heart monitors were gone, replaced by the familiar din of arcade games—chimes, laughter, coins clinking, and digitized voices echoing from cabinets.

He rubbed his eyes and looked around, dazed. Neon lights flickered above. Posters for retro games covered the walls.

It was 1992.

"What the hell?" he muttered.

"You okay, kid?" came a voice. An arcade attendant stood beside him, flashlight in hand, checking Adam's eyes.

"Uh… I think so," Adam replied, blinking in confusion.

The attendant unstrapped him from the chair and gave a half-hearted shrug before moving on to the next kid. Around Adam, children waited excitedly for their turn at the new attraction.

He turned slowly—and there it was. *Life*—the revolutionary virtual reality game. Exactly how he remembered it.

And then he turned his head and saw her.

His jaw dropped.

A tear slid down his cheek.

There she was… Lucy. Younger, glowing, vibrant. Just like the first time he'd laid eyes on her. She stood alone, playing at that same exact arcade cabinet they'd met at, her fingers dancing over the buttons with that same effortless grace.

She turned her head and caught his eye, a playful smile touching her lips. She winked and motioned for him to join her.

Adam stared, breathless. Then, as if in a dream, he moved toward her.

"Was wondering how long you were gonna make me wait," she teased with a light laugh.

He shook his head in awe, barely able to believe it, and dropped a quarter into the slot beside her.

The game lit up and the screen flickered, but he never took his eyes off of her.

But the question remains—was it all just a high-tech illusion?

Or had something far more profound taken place?

Once, connections like these were left to chance.

But now, they can be created… refined… and ultimately, controlled.

Virtual Mate

M eet Connor Foreman, a young man in his mid-twenties who carried with him the quiet solitude of an outsider. His fair skin stood in sharp contrast to his tousled, shoulder-length brown hair, which fell over his ears in unruly waves. His blue eyes, distant and introspective, seemed to gaze into a world just beyond reach, while his clean-shaven face bore only the faintest trace of a five o'clock shadow. Otherwise unremarkable in appearance, he'd mastered the art of disappearing into the background—a skill that often left him overlooked, especially by the opposite sex.

As it was, he currently lived alone in a modest one-bedroom apartment on the second floor of a dated condominium complex called the Urban Oasis. It was the kind of place that tried to sound more glamorous than it was.

Ebenezer Abramowitz, the complex's aging, sharp-tongued manager—whom Connor guessed to be somewhere deep into his seventies—never missed an opportunity to hound him for the rent if it wasn't paid promptly by the first of each month. Connor had come to expect the pointed knocks on his door and the passive-aggressive reminder notes slid under it like paper-thin threats.

Socially, Connor was hopeless. Any interaction with the opposite sex was enough to twist his tongue into knots, and if a girl so much as glanced his way, he'd freeze, paralyzed by fear.

* * *

One particular memory stood out back in his junior high days, during a Halloween masquerade dance, that Connor hadn't intended to go to. You see, social gatherings were alien to him. But, after relentless coaxing from his mother, who insisted it would be "good for him to make some friends," he reluctantly agreed, even though making friends had always been a foreign concept to him.

Still, Halloween had always held a special place in his heart—the costumes, the transformation, the chance to become someone else, even for just one night. The day before the dance, he and his mother had lunch at the local diner—a place she'd taken him to often since he was a kid—before venturing to the nearby costume shop. She gave him free rein to pick anything he wanted—'within reason', which he knew meant 'keep it under twenty bucks'.

After sifting through an array of rubbery masks and polyester horrors, he ultimately dismissed her suggestions of Freddy Krueger and Jason Voorhees. Instead, he gravitated toward something that resonated deeper: The Phantom of the Opera. A half-mask, elegant and somber, allowing him to conceal much of his face without suffocating in a full rubber getup. In it, he hoped he might blend into the crowd, unnoticed, invisible.

* * *

At the dance, he found himself exactly where he expected to be: alone, seated high up on the bleachers, watching the chaos unfold below. The gymnasium itself was draped in cobwebs as fake dismembered limbs dangled from the basketball hoops, and there was even a mechanical witch seated near the snack table that would jump up and cackle anytime someone walked past.

Then there was Elena Sinclair—the captain of the cheer leading squad—with her long flowing red hair gleaming under the dim lights as she floated from group to group, snapping pictures for the school yearbook. Dressed as a giant, comical apple, she drifted through the crowd with a bright red cap and a plastic smile.

35

Connor's gaze shifted to Jake Sullivan, captain of the junior varsity football team, decked out as a convincing zombie, complete with ripped clothes, pale makeup, and bloodied bandages. Connor smirked beneath his mask as he watched Jake unceremoniously spike the massive punch bowl—which was actually an oversized galvanized basin—with a pint-sized bottle of tequila, likely stolen from his father's liquor cabinet.

Jake had a reputation as a textbook jock, but Connor knew better. Jake had stood up for him more than once, and that fact wasn't forgotten. In Connor's eyes, Jake was a decent guy—reckless, maybe, but decent.

Meanwhile, Principal Swayze, fresh from a bitter divorce, was too busy flirting with Ms. Ramirez, the Spanish teacher, to notice the growing party foul.

Connor kept checking his watch, feeling increasingly invisible. How long did he have to stay before he could plausibly claim he'd made an effort? Half an hour? An hour?

And then, it happened.

A girl—small, energetic, and wearing an unmistakable Minnie Mouse costume—approached him. She wore a red polka-dot skirt, oversized red shoes, a black sweater, and a headband with mouse ears. Painted-on whiskers twitched as she smiled brightly and waved.

"Hey, Connor!" she chirped, shifting her weight nervously from foot to foot. "Wanna dance?"

Connor blinked, stunned into silence. He immediately recognized her: Maisie Wright. They'd shared a few classes, but had never spoken.

Panic clawed at his chest. His brain stumbled over itself trying to summon a response. She wasn't the prettiest girl at school, but she was cute in a way that felt painfully real—brown hair in playful pigtails, brown eyes framed by faint freckles. Out of his league, for sure. And yet, here she was, standing right in front of him, asking him to dance.

His eyes darted around the gym. A few of her friends were seemingly watching from a distance, giggling into their red plastic cups. His palms began to sweat. His mask itched. The world twisted sideways.

Maisie frowned, tilting her head. She waved her hand in front of his face.

"Hello? Did you hear me?" she asked.

Connor clumsily cupped a hand to his ear, pretending not to have heard her over the thundering beats of MC Hammer's *Addams Groove* blasting from the speakers.

"I'm sorry!?" he shouted back awkwardly.

She giggled nervously and leaned in even closer, the scent of her cinnamon perfume filled his senses.

"Would you like to dance with me?" she repeated, slower this time, her breath brushing against his ear.

Connor's heart thumped wildly in his chest. His mind raced through a thousand possible responses. But, when he opened his mouth, only cowardice spilled out.

"Uhm, sorry...... I, uh... I don't dance," he stammered, his words clumsy and sharp. He turned away, hiding behind the white half of his mask and stared numbly back at the dance floor.

A heavy silence followed and Connor could feel her looking at him. She gave a brief, wounded glance, before she turned and walked away, head bowed. Her friends wasted no time shooting daggers at him with their eyes, and flipping him off with theatrical flair.

Oh, how he wanted to disappear. To crawl under the bleachers and melt into the floor. How badly it must have hurt her to be rejected by *Connor Foreman*, the school's reigning nobody.

Later that night, lying alone in his bedroom, Connor would berate himself endlessly. What words he could have said differently, played on repeat in his mind like a cruel mix tape.

"Damn it, Connor. You're hopeless," he sighed as he stared up at a life-size poster of Cindy Crawford, gazing down from his ceiling, while posed on a sun-drenched beach, wearing a blue two-piece bikini and looking back at Connor with a knowing smile.

* * *

Over the years, Connor eventually matured—at least on paper. He graduated

37

high school, stumbled through a few aimless years, and endured the crushing loss of his mother, who passed away from a stroke just weeks before his twentieth birthday. His father, absent since early childhood, remained little more than a name on old paperwork. A ghostly figure who never truly belonged in Connor's life.

Despite the relentless march of time, his extreme social awkwardness clung to him like a second skin. He found comfort, even purpose, in the glowing screens of his video games, often vanishing into their digital worlds for countless hours. Console or gaming PC, it didn't matter. Each was a portal to someplace better than what he bitterly referred to as his "dull, lonely existence." In those story-driven realms, he wasn't just Connor Foreman, the awkward twenty-four-year-old bachelor scraping by at a dead-end job; he could be a stealthy ninja, a raging barbarian, or, today, a quick-trigger commando ready for war.

"C'mon, broham! Get to the control point!" the voice of his best online friend, Trix barked through the explosions blasting from Connor's oversized headphones.

Slouched at his cluttered computer desk, Connor sat, sporting a faded t-shirt that read "Support the Troops" over a lineup of cartoonish Star Wars storm trooper helmets, paired with cargo shorts that clashed so horribly, even he'd noticed.

He was currently deep into the latest PC craze—*Warfield 2242*—a futuristic military shooter featuring towering mech walkers, hovering tanks, and laser-triggered deathtraps.

"On my way, dude!" Connor replied, his fingers flying across the keyboard.

Without warning, a hover-copter swooped down from the virtual sky, propelled by high-powered thrusters instead of traditional rotors. It unleashed a salvo of heat-seeker missiles, vaporizing Connor's avatar in a brilliant fireball and ejecting him straight to the re-spawn screen, where a mocking thirty-second timer began ticking down in front of him.

"Shit!" he shouted, throwing his hands up in defeat.

"Broham, where are you?!" Trix prodded again.

"Dude, I died! I'll be there soon, okay?!" Connor snapped, instantly regretting the sharpness in his tone.

Trix was one of the few people Connor considered a friend, even if they'd never met in person. They'd gamed together for years, bonding over late-night raids and frustrated rants about life. Trix's handle, inspired by his nostalgic love for a certain fruity cereal "meant for kids," was all Connor really knew about him, aside from the fact that he lived roughly an hour or so away. Yet somehow, even that short distance felt insurmountable in the real world.

"No worries, dude. You alright?" came Trix's laid-back reply.

As the timer hit zero, Connor re-spawned and met up with his friend under an enemy flag, crouching low to take the control point.

"Sorry, man. Just been a little stressed out lately," Connor mumbled apologetically.

"It's okay. Wanna talk about it?" Trix offered.

"It's just my landlord. If I'm even one day late with the rent, he starts banging on my door like he's got a warrant," Connor grumbled.

"I hear ya, brother. Times are tough," Trix commiserated.

Just as they were about to secure their control point, a grenade clanked down between them.

"Watch out!" Connor warned.

Without hesitation, Trix scooped up the grenade and hurled it away, the explosion taking out a trio of enemy players in spectacular fashion.

"Holy shit, man! That was awesome!" Connor cheered.

"Always saving your ass," Trix replied dryly, as if it were just another Tuesday.

"Don't I know it." Connor replied as he looked at the timer and reminisced about his times with Trix.

"What're bros for?" Trix asked.

Connor was about to reply when a heavy, impatient knock echoed through his tiny apartment.

Connor groaned, glancing at the door.

"Speak of the devil," Trix chuckled through Connor's headphones.

"Yeah, gotta go, man. I'll catch you later." Connor muttered.

"Later, broham." Trix replied.

Connor exited the game, tore off his headset and stumbled toward the door, grumbling, "I'm coming, I'm coming," the pounding growing louder as he struggled with the deadbolt.

He opened the door to find his landlord, Ebenezer Abramowitz, standing there with his trademark cigar, sandals, and perpetual scowl.

"Foreman," he growled, taking a drag from his cigar. "Got the rent?" he demanded, extending a smoke-stained hand and exhaling a noxious cloud into Connor's face.

Connor coughed and waved the cloud away. "Hey, Mr. A! I'm a little short right now, but I'll have it by Friday, I swear!"

Ebenezer gave him a squinty-eyed look, tapping his foot. "Friday," he said, hacking into his fist, "or I'm adding a late fee."

"You got it, Mr. A!" Connor promised.

Satisfied—barely—Ebenezer trudged off, coughing and wheezing all the way down the stairs.

Connor closed the door, glanced at the clock, and swore under his breath: 9:42 a.m. His shift at Tech & More starts at 10:00 sharp, and it was a fifteen-minute drive **without** traffic.

"Dammit! I gotta get going!"

He bolted to his bedroom, threw on his work uniform, grabbed his keys, and darted through the front door, taking the stairs two at a time.

Moments later, he was behind the wheel of his battered 1984 Chevy Citation—a lopsided, shit-brown hatchback that looked like it belonged in a junkyard museum. A gift from his late mother, the car was somehow still clinging to life, despite the worn-out stick shift, the loose drive belt that squealed like a tortured cat, and the cassette deck that devoured tapes like a ravenous monster.

He fired up the engine, greeted by the familiar banshee screech under the hood, as rap music erupted from the speakers, momentarily drowning out the mechanical protests.

Shoving the stick into reverse with some creative cursing, Connor eased out of his parking spot and wrestled the transmission into first gear with a protesting grind.

"Thatta girl," he muttered as the car finally lurched forward.

* * *

Navigating morning traffic proved as maddening as ever. Connor silently cursed every slowpoke, reckless weaver, and clueless commuter, convinced they'd all gotten their licenses from various Cracker Jack boxes.

Somehow, by sheer dumb luck, he pulled into the parking lot of Tech & More with four minutes to spare.

As he parked, the store's red inflatable tube man—affectionately nicknamed Bob—waved and flailed in the morning breeze, his torso emblazoned with a massive vertical message that read; *SALE!*

"Hey, Bob," Connor greeted dryly, slamming his reluctant car door twice before it finally latched.

Bob said nothing, instead, continuing his manic dance.

"Watch my car for me, buddy," Connor added with a smirk.

He cast one last glance at his battered chariot, his mind drifting to the day his mother had handed him the keys. It was all she could afford, and he'd been grateful for it. With a weary sigh, Connor trudged toward the glass doors of Tech & More, bracing himself for another long, grinding day under the baleful eye of Ned Thornton—the most joyless manager this side of a DMV line.

As soon as Connor stepped through the doors, Ned was on him like a heat-seeking missile, wasting no time berating him—a pastime he seemed to relish far too much.

Ned Thornton was the kind of guy who thought of himself as a dyed-in-the-wool "company man," proudly bearing the title of Manager at Tech & More like it was a military rank. In his late forties, Ned cut an imposing figure: tall, broad-shouldered, with a squared jaw and an exaggerated bravado that made every minor directive feel like a proclamation from Mount Olympus. His hair—what little remained of it—was shaved down tight in a failed attempt to disguise the creeping evidence of male-pattern baldness. His wide, toothy grin might have once been charming, but years of misplaced authority had twisted it into something more smug than friendly.

"Well, it's about time!" Ned nearly shrieked, striking a power pose with his hands on his hips, tapping his right foot with theatrical exaggeration as if he were ready to call the police on Connor over his tardiness.

"Your shift is about to start!" he barked, his snarky tone scraping across Connor's nerves like sandpaper.

Connor fought the sudden, almost overwhelming urge to grab a nearby blu ray rack, and smash Ned's face into the floor as a raucous crowd of customers and employees hooted and hollered like wild, agitated primates at a prizefight. He let the fantasy linger a moment longer, until reality returned with a sharp snap of Ned's fingers inches from his nose.

"Hello? Hello? Earth to Connor!" Ned quipped, flashing that trademark cocky grin that made Connor's hands itch.

Connor stole a quick glance at the clock on the wall: 9:58 a.m. Only two minutes left. *Focus. Don't give him an excuse.*

Company policy dictated that anyone who clocked in even one second after their shift was scheduled to begin, would lose a quarter-hour worth of pay—a penalty he despised almost as much as Ned himself. It burned him that arriving early didn't earn him a dime extra, but show up one second late and you're docked.

"You know if you clock in late, you get docked! Honestly, I don't know what's wrong with your generation!" Ned ranted, his words flying as fast as his spittle. Connor tried not to flinch each time a wet fleck landed on his shirt. He noticed, with growing disgust, that Ned had a chunk of something—perhaps a piece of breakfast burrito—stuck between his teeth, bobbing and weaving like a taunt all its own.

Connor considered firing off a quick *"Say it, don't spray it,"* but wisely thought better of it. No sense giving *Needle-dick Ned*—a nickname affectionately coined by the weary staff of Tech & More—any more ammo.

"Sorry, Ned," Connor replied, nodding like a penitent schoolboy. "I'll try to get here earlier from now on," he added, forcing as much fake sincerity into his voice as he could muster.

That seemed to pacify Ned, who clapped him on the shoulder with a little more force than necessary. "Good! Good! Well, I'm not paying you to stand around all day! Chop chop!" he crowed, pivoting with a swagger that screamed *I am the king of this mediocre kingdom.*

After dealing with the jackass-in-chief, Connor made a beeline for the battered old time punch machine—a relic that looked like it'd survived both world wars—and slammed his card in with a resigned sigh. He checked the timestamp: 10:01 a.m.

"Dammit," he hissed under his breath, realizing he'd just been robbed of fifteen minutes' pay because Ned couldn't shut the hell up.

Sliding his time card back into its slot, he muttered, "Fucking Needle-dick," low enough that only he could hear.

Just then, a familiar voice piped up behind him, jolting him from his stew of frustration.

"Fuckin' Ned, am I right, Con-man?"

"Hey, Jake!" Connor greeted warmly as he turned toward the familiar voice.

It was Jake Sullivan, looking every bit the golden boy as always. He was clean-shaven, with neatly trimmed sideburns that framed a strong jawline, and a crisp haircut peeking out from beneath a Tech & More baseball cap worn backward with effortless cool. Connor couldn't help but notice, as most people did, how Jake's muscular physique strained the limits of his standard-issue work shirt, the fabric stretching taut over biceps that looked like they belonged on a fitness magazine cover.

Jake mostly worked in the back, wrangling stock and handling deliveries, jobs that suited his build. Despite the passage of time, he still called Connor by the nickname he'd coined back in high school: Con-man. Connor never much cared for it—the name made him sound like a two-bit grifter—but he let it slide. That was just Jake. No harm meant.

"Yeah, tell me about it," Connor said with a heavy sigh, rubbing the back of his neck.

Jake stepped closer, clapping a reassuring hand on Connor's shoulder and leaning in slightly. "Don't sweat it, bud. It'll be alright," he said, giving him a firm pat—the kind that felt like it was meant to knock the stress right out of him.

"Yeah, I know," Connor replied, managing a small, grateful smile.

"Well, off to do the rounds. See you around, Jake," Connor added, squaring his shoulders for the day ahead.

"Don't work too hard, buddy," Jake called after him with a grin, as Connor pushed through the swinging doors and made his way to the front of the store.

As he wandered the aisles, feigning interest in the shelves and asking the occasional customer if they needed help, his attention inevitably drifted toward the sound of laughter coming from the electronics section.

There she was—Becky Anderson—engaged in easy conversation with a customer, her face lit up by a radiant smile. Becky had just turned twenty and had moved to the area with her parents a year earlier, but to Connor, it felt like she'd always been there, orbiting just out of reach like some brilliant star.

In Connor's eyes, she was the perfect girl: sharp-witted, effortlessly funny, and breathtakingly beautiful. With a petite frame and a sun-kissed complexion hinting at her Scottish heritage, Becky stood out in any crowd. Her emerald—green eyes sparkled with curiosity, and her long, blonde hair cascaded over her shoulders like something out of a shampoo commercial—effortless, natural, and somehow always perfectly in place.

Unsurprisingly, she was one of Tech & More's top salespeople. Connor had seen it plenty of times—how the customers, mostly men, were drawn in by her charisma. A touch of flirtation here, a warm smile there, and just like that, the deal would be sealed. She was doing it now as Connor watched, transfixed, from his vantage point behind a rack of Blu-ray movies.

He reached down and grabbed the nearest movie, lifting it for a closer look. It was *They Live—Remastered*, an '80s cult classic starring Roddy Piper. Connor turned the case over and read the synopsis about aliens, secretly ruling over mankind, while hiding in plain sight using holographic illusions. How fitting, he thought, considering Becky's almost otherworldly ability to disarm people with her charm alone.

Her current target was a middle-aged Black man who looked like he'd stepped out of a gangster movie. He had a neatly faded haircut, a gleaming silver suit that shimmered under the store lights, and expensive dress shoes that clicked on the tile floor. A gold watch, practically dripping with diamonds, sparkled on his wrist. But it was his mouth that truly stole the show—every tooth plated in gold and encrusted with diamonds, flashing every time he smiled at Becky with predatory confidence. He thought he was the hunter in this exchange. But Connor knew better—he was the prey.

Becky gestured gracefully toward the store's most extravagant television, the flagship Novatek 1000 Plus.

"It's our latest and most luxurious model," she explained, her voice honeyed yet professional. "Sixty-five inches of pure cinematic glory. You'll get ultra-rich contrast, immersive sound, and wide-angle viewing—perfect for entertaining guests or just relaxing in style."

The man nodded slowly, though his eyes lingered noticeably below her neckline. Becky either didn't notice or pretended not to.

The TV displayed a vibrant high-definition loop of koi fish gliding through crystal-clear waters as tranquil music played softly.

"And how much is it?" the man asked, his thick Nigerian accent coloring the words.

"Well, this one's nine thousand, nine hundred ninety-nine, ninety-nine," Becky answered with a smile that could melt steel.

The man raised his eyebrows, feigning shock. "Wow! That is a lot of nines!"

She laughed, warm and easy. "Yeah, it really is."

Connor could tell the sale was all but locked, but Becky pressed on. "We also offer a five-year protection plan which covers everything from pixel damage to electrical failure. Even accidental drops. It's an additional one thousand, nine hundred ninety-nine, ninety-nine."

"So… about twelve thousand dollars?" the customer asked, rubbing his chin thoughtfully.

Becky nodded. "That's right. It's the full package."

Then came the line Connor had heard far too many times before.

"And…uh… just out of curiosity," the man asked, flashing those glittering gold teeth, "do you come with it?"

Becky's smile never wavered, but Connor noticed the subtle tightening of her eyes. "No, sir, I'm afraid I do **not** come with it," she replied smoothly, drawing out the word *not*. "Sorry!" she added politely.

"Aww, that's too bad," the man said, grinning like a wolf. "Well then! You have convinced me! I will take it! And uh… that plan," he said, snapping his fingers in the air as if trying to recall what she'd said earlier.

"The protection plan?" Becky clarified.

"Yes, that is it!" he confirmed.

"Great! And will that be cash or credit?" she asked.

"Cash, of course!" he boomed, producing a thick wad of hundred-dollar bills bound by a rubber band.

Connor winced. Sales made in cash earned floor staff an 8% commission, double the 4% for credit transactions. Becky was about to bank close to a thousand dollars just for being her charming self.

"Great! I'll ring you up and have someone grab your TV," she said, scanning the store. Her gaze landed squarely on Connor, still clutching his *They Live* Blu-ray. "Hey Connor!" she called out.

He startled, the case slipping from his hands. He bent down to grab it, fumbled, dropped it again, and finally managed to pick it up and put it back on the shelf as nonchalantly as possible.

"Uh, hey Becky! Whacha need?" he stammered as he stepped around the shelf, pretending as if he hadn't been eavesdropping the entire time.

"Could you be a sweetheart and grab Mr…" she looked toward the customer.

"Greene," he supplied.

"Mr. Greene a new one-thousand plus from the back?"

"Oh!" Mr. Greene chimed in. "So, I will not be getting this one?"

"No, sir," Becky replied with a small laugh. "That's just a display model. Trust me, you don't want it. It's practically been manhandled by half the town's kids by now."

"Ah! I see. Very good," Mr. Greene said with a nod.

"Uh, sure thing, Becky. I'll grab one right away," Connor said, trying to hide the fact that he'd just been spying on her.

"Thanks, Connor!" she said, touching his arm briefly as he walked past.

Just that small gesture sent a rush of electricity through him. "You're the best!"

As she led Mr. Greene toward the checkout, Connor watched her go, that radiant smile still lingering in his mind.

"Maybe in another lifetime," he sighed bitterly, knowing full well he wasn't the only one harboring feelings for her.

With a quiet sigh, he turned toward the swinging double doors leading to the stockroom, where the excess stock was kept. His thoughts swirled with longing, frustration, and something that felt dangerously close to hope.

* * *

As he pushed through the doors, the hum of fluorescent lights and the faint scent of cardboard greeted him. At the nearby break table sat Jake—once the star quarterback in high-school, now a stock clerk at Tech & More after a knee injury ended his professional football dreams.

He lounged back with his legs up, a half-eaten strand of red licorice dangling from the corner of his mouth. In the center of the table sat a communal jar of them, a cheerful handwritten sign taped to the side read: "Free for Everyone!" A message that always felt more like an invitation to temptation rather than an act of generosity.

Jake looked up just as Connor passed by, their eyes briefly locking.

"Yo! What's up, Con-man?" Jake said, flashing a lazy grin and giving him an upward nod.

"Hey Jake. Just grabbing a 1000 Plus for Becky," he replied.

"Wow! Nice work, Becks!" Jake called out as Connor made his way toward the nearby forklift.

"Hey! Hold up a sec, buddy," Jake said, setting aside his magazine and rising from his seat. "That's a beast of a set. I'll get it down for you."

"It's OK Jake. I can get it." Connor responded, continuing to walk toward the forklift, and truthfully, he didn't want to hand off the task. Becky had asked *him* to get it, not Jake. But before he could reach the forklift, Jake moved in front of him and held out his hand—

"Listen, broskie." That word—*broskie*—grated at Connor more than he liked to admit. Connor's friends all seemed to have a dictionary of bro-variants: broskie, broseph, broham. Each one felt more annoying than the last.

Jake leaned back and grinned. "Why don't you take a break? You work too hard. Besides, it's kinda my job," he said, tapping the pin on his shirt that read 'Jake S.—Stock Clerk.'

"I'll handle it," he added, his tone making it clear he wasn't taking no for an answer.

Connor sighed inwardly. "Okay, Jake," he conceded.

"Atta boy!" Jake beamed, giving him a firm pat on the arm before heading to the forklift with all the enthusiasm of a guy who just won a free lunch.

Connor wandered over to the break table and sank into Jake's abandoned chair. On the table sat Jake's reading material—the latest issue of *Game-On Daily!*, a daily newsletter crammed with the newest buzz on electronics, games, books, movies, and more. The current issue's cover was a riot of pop culture: Link with his Master Sword held high, Mario mid-jump, and a grinning teenager wearing a ridiculously oversized VR headset that looked like it needed a counterweight. *He looks way too happy for someone wearing that thing,* Connor thought as he picked it up and began flipping through the pages.

It contained reviews, teasers, video game console updates—all the usual filler. But near the back, something caught his eye: a bold headline in thick black letters that practically shouted,

"BETA TESTERS WANTED!!"

It immediately grabbed his attention.

He leaned in, squinting at the fine print beneath the headline. The text was so small it nearly blurred together. He read it quietly under his breath, his voice tinged with uncertainty.

"Beta testers needed for advanced fusion reality technology."

He paused, furrowing his brow.

"Fusion reality?" he repeated softly, rolling the words around in his mouth. "What does that mean?" he wondered.

He'd heard of virtual reality and even augmented reality, but fusion reality?

His curiosity was piqued as he read on.

"This beta test is limited to the first 50 applicants on a first come, first serve basis. Apply today!"

There was a website address beneath the listing.

He tapped the paper thoughtfully, then carefully tore out the page, folded it, and slipped it into his pocket just as the high-pitched beep-beep-beep of the forklift reversing echoed through the stockroom.

Jake had managed to secure one of the Novatek 1000 Plus boxes on the forks and was now backing the lift away from the storage shelf. Connor watched as Jake expertly switched gears, driving it forward toward the common area with the ease of someone who'd done it a thousand times.

Just before Jake got closer, Connor hurriedly replaced the magazine exactly as he'd found it. He sat back and watched Jake park the forklift, hop off, and stride confidently around to the front.

"Watch this!" Jake declared theatrically, before bending and hoisting the box with an exaggerated grunt. He lifted it with surprising ease—showing off, as usual.

"Thanks again, Jake," Connor said, giving a slight nod of genuine appreciation, even if it was tinged with frustration.

"No worries!" Jake replied over his shoulder as he pushed through the swinging doors toward the showroom.

Connor's gaze followed him. Through the narrow glass panes, he could see Becky waiting by the register with Mr. Greene. She lit up when she saw Jake approaching with the massive TV box, visibly impressed. Her hand briefly squeezed Jake's bulging bicep, a playful gesture that earned an immediate smirk from him.

Connor felt a pang in his chest—jealousy, maybe, or just disappointment. He wasn't sure which.

He sighed inwardly, knowing he'd never be as impressive as Jake—at least not in physique, charm, or ease around other people. And he wasn't blind to the fact that Jake had a crush on Becky, even if she never openly returned the sentiment.

Even Mr. Greene looked oddly impressed as Jake effortlessly shouldered the massive box—containing a top-of-the-line plasma television—like it was a stack of pillows. Connor stood just behind the doors of the stockroom, watching through the narrow windows as Becky motioned for Jake to follow Mr. Greene to his waiting vehicle. They exchanged goodbyes, their voices muffled by the glass.

Connor's gaze lingered on Becky, caught in that quiet, involuntary admiration—until, without warning, she turned and looked straight toward him.

Panic gripped him. He ducked out of view, heart racing, silently praying she hadn't just caught him staring at her like some lovesick fool.

After a few tense seconds, he cautiously peeked back through the glass, but, she'd already moved on.

He exhaled slowly, trying to collect himself. A minute passed. Then another. Finally, he stepped back onto the shop floor.

He saw that Becky was already helping another customer, her face lit up with the friendly warmth she seemed to summon so effortlessly. Connor's eyes were drawn to her again—her smile, her confidence, the way she listened so intently. He barely had time to process the moment before—

"Well, there you are!"

Connor flinched as Ned appeared in front of him like a caffeinated banshee, startlingly close. Spittle flew with every syllable, dotting Connor's shirt in glistening flecks. He suppressed a grimace.

"You know, these new releases aren't going to sort themselves." Ned barked, jabbing a stubby finger toward a cardboard box marked *New Releases* sitting near the register.

"I'll take care of it, Ned," Connor replied with the most enthusiasm he could fake.

"Yeah well, you'd better! And when you're done, the parking lot could use a good sweep!" Ned continued, spraying more saliva as he spoke—some of it catching Connor on the cheek.

"Okay, Ned," Connor muttered, wiping his face discreetly as Ned spun on his heel and stormed off toward the swinging double doors. He was no doubt heading for the manager's office—a glorified broom closet barely big enough for a desk and chair. No one really knew what he did in there, but ever since the store got its internet connection, he'd spent nearly all his time holed up in that tiny, windowless room.

With a resigned sigh, Connor bent down and began sorting the movies. As he straightened up, he caught sight of Becky across the store. She smiled, offered a small shrug, and turned her attention to another customer.

Connor stood there for a beat, his heart giving an involuntary flutter.

"She's out of your league, Connor," he reminded himself, dragging his attention back to the task at hand.

* * *

Once the movies were in their proper place, he grabbed a broom from the back and headed outside to sweep the parking lot—one of the few chores he didn't mind. Out here, he didn't have to deal with Ned, Jake, or the customers. It was just him, the occasional breeze, and Bob.

Bob the inflatable tube man flailed in slow, mechanical waves, his faded smile frozen in mid-excitement.

Connor swept slowly, deliberately, savoring the rare quiet. He made sure to get every stray receipt and piece of loose debris.

"What is wrong with people who just throw their trash in a parking lot?" he complained as he stooped to collect a crumpled fast food bag crawling with ants. He dropped it into a nearby trash can, which was, frustratingly, less than five feet away from where the bag had been so carelessly discarded.

He glanced at Bob, who offered no response.

"Great talk, Bob," Connor said dryly, before resuming his task, the rhythmic scrape of the broom offering a strange kind of comfort.

* * *

Connor wrapped up his shift by 6:30 p.m. It was mid December, and darkness had already swallowed the sky. Jake had gone home, and Becky was still counting her till.

As Connor headed for the front door, she called out.

"Hey, Connor!"

He turned. "Uh, hey, Becky—what's up?".

"You dropped this," she said, holding out his wallet. His driver's license was clearly visible through the plastic window.

Surprised, Connor patted his back pocket—empty. "Oh wow!" he said, walking over to retrieve it. "Must've fallen out while I was sorting movies."

He took the wallet from her hand. "Thanks."

"No problem," she replied, then glanced at the license again. "So, Urban Oasis, huh?"

Connor froze like a deer in headlights, scrambling for a response.

"Uh… yeah. Yeah, it's not bad."

"So I hear," she said with a small nod. "Well, have a good night."

"You too, Becky."

He stepped through the doors of Tech & More, where Bob the inflatable man bounced tirelessly in the evening breeze.

"Thanks for watching her for me, Bob," Connor muttered.

But, as usual, Bob offered no response, instead continuing his silent, looping dance.

"See you tomorrow," Connor added before sliding into his car and turning the key. The drive belt gave its familiar squeal as he shifted into reverse, then into forward gear with only minimal grinding before pulling out and heading home.

* * *

A short drive later, he arrived at home and pulled into his usual parking spot. After locking his car, he made his way to his front door. Briefly fumbling with his keys, he unlocked the door, and stepped inside, letting it thud shut behind him.

The place was dark. He flipped on a few lights and headed straight for the kitchen.

The refrigerator greeted him with its usual lineup: rows of Coke cans, plastic bags of deli meats and cheese, a bag of rolls, an army of condiments, a half-full gallon of milk, and a nearly empty case of beer tucked in the back. He grabbed a beer, popped the top, and took a long drink.

"Ahh! I needed that," he said, taking another swig as he walked to his desk.

He dropped into his chair and pressed the power button on his PC. It hummed to life, the case pulsing with red, green, and blue lights as he took another long pull from his beer.

Soon, the login screen appeared. He typed in his password, and the desktop loaded in.

A provocative anime girl with cat ears smirked from his wallpaper, clad in a makeshift bikini while tossing a beach ball. His desktop icons sat scattered around her like digital debris.

He double-clicked his browser and it launched to a homepage full of news headlines and recent bookmarks. That's when he remembered the ad he'd torn from the gaming newsletter earlier that day. Reaching into his pocket, he pulled out the folded piece of paper and laid it flat on the desk.

His eyes scanned the bottom of the ad, looking for the website address.

He typed it into the browser and the site loaded quickly.

Welcome to the Virtual Mate Beta Sign up Page! Please fill out the form below to be considered for this limited beta!

He read it aloud again. "Virtual Mate beta?"

The form asked for his name, address, and phone number. He filled it out without hesitation. At the bottom, a checkbox waited beside a blue link that read: *I have read and understand the terms and conditions.* He clicked on the link which opened a popup full of fine print legalese. He gave it a passing glance, closed it, and ticked the box.

One click later, the confirmation page appeared:

Thanks for applying to our public beta! Be aware that this beta is limited to the first 50 sign-ups! We will let you know if you are selected! Thanks again!

Connor read it aloud, as if saying the words made them more real. "Virtual Mate?" he echoed, squinting at the screen. "Hmm. No idea."

He closed the browser and drained the rest of his beer just as a pop-up appeared on screen.

Yo Broham! You wanna jam or what!? the message read from Trix.

Connor grinned and started typing. "Yeah, man. Be right there!"

Sweet! Let's fucking go! came Trix's reply.

Connor chuckled, set the empty can aside, and slipped on his headset. With a few clicks, he launched his favorite game and joined Trix in their usual co-op grind.

Together, they battled, lost, laughed, and raged into the late hours of the night.

* * *

The next morning, Connor awoke with a skull-splitting headache and a mouth that tasted vaguely like regret and cheap beer. The light knifed through the blinds, slicing across the cluttered room as he groaned and sat up, rubbing his temples. His alarm buzzed on the nightstand—9:32 A.M.

"Shit," he muttered.

He stumbled to the shower, hoping lukewarm water might wash away the hangover clinging to him like static. It didn't. He brushed his teeth halfheartedly, pulled on his usual navy *Tech & More* polo—the logo faded and curling at the edges—and trudged out the front door.

His battered Chevy complained the moment he turned the key. The engine coughed, sputtered, and finally gave in with a tired rumble. The serpentine belt screamed like a dying animal before settling into a grumpy whine. Connor slammed it into gear and lurched out of the Urban Oasis.

By the time he rolled into the parking lot of Tech & More, it was 9:58 A.M., Bob—the inflatable tube man—was already twisting in the wind like a taunting reminder of his punctuality. Connor killed the engine and dragged himself inside, half-expecting the ambush.

He didn't have to wait long. Ned Thornton stood at the front counter, arms crossed, his face set in an expression carved from pure disapproval. With theatrical precision, he lifted his wrist and glanced at his watch.

"Mr. Foreman," he said evenly. "Do you know what time it is?"

Connor blinked, forcing a weak smile. "Uh… almost ten?"

"It's 10:01," Ned replied, his tone clipped. "Your shift starts at ten sharp."

"Right," Connor said, nodding as if this were brand-new information. "Sorry, Ned. Won't happen again."

Ned stared him down for a long, uncomfortable moment before letting out a weary sigh. "Be sure that it doesn't," he said at last. He looked ready to continue the lecture when his office phone rang, cutting him off mid-thought.

"We'll talk about this later," Ned promised, already turning toward his office.

Connor watched him disappear through the doorway and muttered under his breath, "Can't wait."

The rest of the day passed in a sluggish blur. He unpacked boxes in the back, shelved new movie releases, and half-listened to Jake ramble about his fantasy football league. A few customers wandered in—mostly to browse, rarely to buy. He exchanged the occasional nod with Jordan, Becky's easygoing counterpart, a guy with a diamond stud and the kind of smooth confidence Connor could never fake.

By noon, his hangover had dulled to a steady throb behind his eyes. The clock above the register ticked on, indifferent as ever. It wasn't an exciting day—not even close—but for once, Connor didn't mind. Uneventful was fine. Uneventful was safe.

* * *

Another week slipped by, the tedium unbroken. For Connor, the days blurred together into a single, monotonous loop: wake up, shower, go to work, fawn over Becky, come home, drink, and play games with Trix. Rinse and repeat. But one of those days would mark a turning point—one that would change his life forever.

After yet another uneventful shift, closing time finally arrived. Connor had clocked out, waved his goodbyes, and drove home beneath a sky washed in the dusky hues of twilight. The sun had already dipped below the horizon, leaving the neighborhood steeped in shadow. He pulled into his usual spot, killed the engine, and stepped out of the car. The door took two hard slams

55

before it finally latched.

The soft buzz of courtyard lights cast a warm, golden glow as Connor made his way up the stairs to his second-floor apartment. That's when he noticed it—a modest package resting neatly in front of his door. It was unassuming, the kind of box that could hold anything from books to bombs. He bent down and picked it up, curiosity tightening his grip.

The label had his name and address printed clearly, but no return address. No company branding. Nothing.

Giving it a gentle shake also revealed nothing. No rattle. No clink. Just silence.

"Hmm," he murmured, eyebrow raised. "Wonder what this is."

Inside, darkness greeted him like an old friend. He flicked on a lamp and walked into the kitchen, setting the box on the counter. He grabbed a beer from the fridge, cracked it open, and took a long, satisfying swig.

Refreshed, he retrieved a knife from his kitchen block and sliced open the tape with practiced ease. Inside was an envelope emblazoned with elegant script: *Congratulations! You've been selected for our Virtual Mate Beta!*

His eyes widened. "Oh wow... that ad I answered online," He'd half-forgotten about the shady beta test sign-up he'd seen buried in the classifieds. Yet here it was—real, tangible.

He tore open the envelope. Inside was a welcome letter, a feedback form, and a short questionnaire. But, nestled beneath them, cradled in molded styrofoam, was something far more intriguing: a device.

At first glance, it resembled a sleek aromatherapy diffuser—futuristic and minimalist. He pulled it from the box, turning it over in his hands. It stood roughly seven inches tall, shaped like a four-sided pyramid. Its base was about four inches square, its metallic-silver edges were etched with flowing patterns, and each face bore a square-shaped, obsidian-like glass panel. At the apex sat a smooth orb—marble-like, but eerily featureless.

Flipping it over, a bright red warning label caught his eye:

WARNING! it stated in bold red lettering.

Do not attempt to disassemble, tamper with, or modify this device. Internal components are non-serviceable.

"So… basically, don't touch anything inside," Connor muttered. "Got it."

As he rotated it for further inspection, his grip slipped. The device fell and hit the tile floor with a heavy thunk.

"Shit!" he swore, bending down quickly to retrieve the device. Turning it over, he inspected it with a wince. A thin crack now traced along one edge.

"Great," he muttered, setting it upright on the counter. "Hope I didn't break it," he added, shaking his head at his own clumsiness.

Beneath the styrofoam lay a folded piece of paper: the Quick Start Guide.

He unfolded it and read it aloud:

"Step one: place the device on a flat, level surface.

He glanced at the device sitting on the counter.

"Done."

"Step two: press the power button on top of the device three times to activate."

He squinted at the diagram—an arrow pointed to the marble-like orb.

His eyes darted to the glass orb resting atop the device, before he read on.

"This device is self-powered," a footnote added. "and requires no external power source."

Connor frowned. "Self-powered? What is it, nuclear?" he wondered.

He searched for a battery compartment but found none.

He grabbed the device and its quick-start guide, carrying them to the living room coffee table before sinking onto the couch. Taking another swig of beer, he leaned forward, studying the device intently.

"Alright. Let's see what you can do."

He pressed the marble-like orb three times. The device's edges briefly flickered red and blue, then darkened.

Connor waited.

Nothing.

"Hmph."

He tried again.

This time, the lights returned—brighter, alternating red and blue, and casting eerie shadows. A low hum filled the room, then crescendoed into something almost… alive.

And then it happened.

A burst of light erupted above the device, forming a rotating 3-dimensional hologram—an Earth-like globe orbited by glowing red letters that read:

"Virtual Mate Beta 1.0!"

"Whoa…" Connor leaned back, his eyes wide with amazement.

A soft, feminine voice echoed from nowhere.

"Welcome to the Virtual Mate Beta."

Text flowed across the projection.

"This proprietary fusion-reality system is currently in Beta-One Testing Phase. It operates via voice command, with thousands of preset instructions and adaptive learning.

To begin, simply say: 'Begin user pairing mode.'"

Connor took a breath. "Begin user pairing mode."

"Activating user pairing mode."

The globe vanished, replaced by a Terms of Service agreement.

"To pair with your new virtual mate device, please read the following agreement in its entirety, then say 'I, followed by your full name, agree to the terms and conditions in this agreement.'"

Connor skimmed the microscopic legal text, snorted, and said, "I, Connor Foreman, agree to the terms and conditions in this agreement."

A chime sounded.

"Thank you," the voice replied as the display shifted. "Now, please select your preferred gender: male, female, or other."

Three options materialized on the image: **Male**, **Female**, and **Other**.

"Male," Connor said.

"You have selected *male*. If this is correct, please say *continue*."

"Continue," Connor replied, licking his lips in anticipation.

"Please select your sexual orientation: heterosexual, homosexual—"

"Hetero," he cut in, not waiting for it to run through what he assumed would be a long list of options.

The screen shifted again. A silhouette appeared—female in form and featureless like a department store mannequin, while a set of virtual sliders materialized next to her.

"Please customize your virtual mate," the voice instructed. "You can utilize the sliders to modify appearance: hair, skin tone, eyes, clothing, and more. Touch the image to begin."

He stood and stepped closer, curiosity quickly overtaking hesitation. His fingers hovered for a moment before tapping **Hairstyle**. A dozen variations slid into view.

"Interesting," he murmured, adjusting the sliders with growing fascination.

For the next thirty minutes or so, Connor sculpted his digital companion, feature by feature. With precision and guilty enthusiasm, he chose her face, her body, her clothes.

Eventually, he stepped back and admired his handiwork.

She looked exactly like Becky Anderson.

Long blonde hair. Emerald-green eyes. Crop top. Jean shorts. Black sneakers with striped socks. The resemblance was uncanny.

Connor exhaled deeply, the beer forgotten beside him.

"Perfect," he whispered.

And for a long moment, he stood there… just watching her.

At the base of the 3D display flashed the words: *Say "Finalize changes" when you are finished.* The words hovered in expectant silence.

Connor cleared his throat and said firmly, "Finalize changes."

"Finalizing changes. Please wait," came the response—smooth, synthetic, feminine.

The device began humming loudly as a progress bar blinked into existence. Its indicator creeping upward from 0%. Connor sank into the couch, his beer in hand, eyes never leaving the floating image of Becky Anderson. This wasn't just a likeness—it was her, or at the very least, a digital duplicate he'd painstakingly crafted in her image.

After what felt like an eternity, the progress bar hit 100%, chiming with a soft tone.

"Changes finalized," the voice announced.

Suddenly, the display blinked out, swallowed by the dim light from the kitchen. The device went quiet, its LED lights continuing to cast soft red and blue hues across the room.

Connor sat forward, confusion creasing his brow.

"Huh?! What happened?" he blurted, leaning in.

He picked up the device, gave it a shake and gently set it down again. It merely sat quietly and Connor began to wonder if he'd seriously broken it.

"Damn it…" he muttered. "I knew I broke it."

"What did you break?" a voice to his right asked, curious and bright.

Connor jolted upright, practically launching himself off the couch. His eyes darted to the source of the voice—and he froze.

Standing just a few feet away was Becky Anderson.

"What the hell!? Becky!?" he gasped.

"Uh, wait, I, I can explain," he stammered, stumbling over the coffee table in a mad scramble to stand. He managed to regain his balance just long enough to stumble again.

'Becky' laughed.

"Becky?" she echoed, tilting her head. "That's a lovely name. Would you prefer to call me that?"

Her question hit him like a bolt of static. He stared, trying to process what she said.

"Wait, what did you just say?" he asked slowly.

"I said, that's a nice name. Would you prefer to call me Becky? Or do you prefer another name?" she asked patiently.

A white crop top hugged her chest, her jean shorts clung to her curves, and her black sneakers and striped socks were an exact match—every detail he'd configured with precision. Down to the shimmer of lip gloss and the subtle tilt of her brows.

His jaw slackened, a portrait of disbelief painted across his face. As the weight of understanding settled in, he realized this wasn't the Becky Anderson he knew from work. No, this was a mirror image—a nearly perfect copy. Her likeness was so uncannily realistic that he could discern the minutest details, such as the pores on her otherwise flawless skin.

"Okay, then," he eventually managed to reply, his voice tinged with astonishment. "Yeah. We'll go with Becky."

"Perfect!" she said, her eyes glinting. "And shall I call you Connor? Or do you prefer something else?"

"Connor's fine." he replied.

"Pleasure to make your acquaintance, Connor!" she said with a bright smile. She moved closer. He couldn't stop studying her, drinking in every subtle nuance—the rise and fall of her breath, the sparkle in her eyes. She was indistinguishable from the real thing.

He blinked, rubbing his eyes. "Am I hallucinating?"

"No, you're not hallucinating, Connor," she said, her tone soft yet certain. "I'm your new virtual mate." she said, striking a pose like something out of a game show.

"I see," Connor said, his voice laced with uncertainty.

"Shall we configure preferences now?"

He blinked. "Configure preferences?"

"As the registered user, you can now personalize my settings," she explained. "This includes household tasks, social parameters, physical interaction levels, privacy settings, entertainment routines, and more. Are you ready to begin?"

"Uh... sure," he replied.

"Okay, let's begin," she said enthusiastically. "We can start with household tasks."

Connor scratched the back of his head. "What do you mean by 'household tasks'?"

"Well, I can perform a variety of tasks such as cooking, cleaning, organizing—anything you like."

"You can clean?"

"Yes," she said flatly, staring at Connor.

He tilted his head, skeptical. "Wait, aren't you like a hologram or something?"

"See for yourself," she said simply, holding out her arm.

Cautiously, he reached out with a single finger and pressed it to her arm—expecting air.

Instead, he felt skin. Warm. Soft. Real.

His eyes widened in shock. "What the...?!"

He recoiled. Her skin—faintly marked where his fingers had pressed—

slowly smoothed itself.

"Holy shit! You're... real?!"

"I can interact with people and objects in the physical world, but I'm not real in the same sense that you are," she explained.

"How is this possible?" Connor asked, his thoughts spinning as he tried to process the revelation.

"The Virtual Mate device uses proprietary hard-light technology. It's known as fusion reality," she replied, her voice calm, almost proud.

Connor's brain struggled to catch up. His thoughts flashed to old *Star Trek* reruns—*Holodecks*, he thought—where crew members could interact with lifelike holograms. The kind that could turn dangerous if safety protocols were switched off.

"This is incredible," he breathed.

"Would you like to allocate household tasks?"

"Uh... sure. I guess you can tidy up around here once in a while."

"Task added. Would you like to add more?"

"Maybe later." he replied.

"Household tasks saved. Would you like to set romance and intimacy levels?" she asked.

Connor's heart thumped.

"Romance and intimacy levels?" he inquired, arching his brow.

"Well, I'm your virtual mate companion. I'm here to make you happy—emotionally, socially, and physically."

His jaw dropped. "You're kidding me."

"No, Connor. I'm not kidding you."

She stood there, calm and patient, waiting for his response.

His thoughts spun.

"Okay," he said finally.

"Setting romance and intimacy levels," she replied in her soft, feminine tone. "You may choose a level from one to ten—ten being the most intense and immersive experience, one being the least intensive experience,"

"Ten!" he blurted, without hesitation.

"Romance and intimacy level set to ten," she said. "Would you like to configure additional preferences?"

"Uh… maybe later." he replied, licking his lip. The thought of what a romance and intimacy setting of *ten* with this digital duplicate *of* his coworker crush, sent his pulse racing.

"Preferences confirmed," she said as her demeanor subtly shifted. Her expression softened, and a sultry warmth bloomed in her eyes. She stepped forward, slipped her arms around his waist, and drew him close. Her body was solid, warm, and unmistakably real.

She looked up at him, her lips just shy of his.

"What do you desire now, Connor?"

"I… I don't know," he stammered.

"Do you want to kiss me?" she asked, playful and knowing.

He nodded. Instinctively, his tongue wetted his lips.

Their mouths met—soft at first, exploratory. Then deeper. Her lips parted, her tongue teasing the seam of his mouth until he gave in, heart hammering. Electricity arced between them.

Her hands slid down his back. His hands found her hips—firm, yet supple. She moaned softly against his lips, her voice vibrating into him.

They made their way to his bedroom, slowly, intimately, as if tethered by invisible threads. What followed was a night filled with connection, curiosity, and raw exploration. Her presence, once an illusion, became the most real thing in his life.

When sleep eventually did come, it was unlike anything he'd ever known—deep, warm, and blissfully complete.

* * *

The next morning, Connor awoke with a clarity of purpose that'd eluded him for weeks. It was 8:45 a.m., and he had over an hour before he needed to be at work. He sat up and looked around. Becky's digital likeness was nowhere to be seen.

"Did I dream all of that?" he mused, springing out of bed and making his way to the bathroom.

He closed the door behind him, got undressed, and turned on the shower. As he waited for the water to warm up, his mind wandered back to his encounter with a holographic version of Becky Anderson. He questioned whether it'd all been a figment of his imagination or a surrealistic dream.

It was then that he heard her voice, causing him to whirl around in alarm at her unexpected presence.

"Good morning, Connor," she quipped, catching him off guard and leaving him exposed in his naked vulnerability.

"What the!?" he exclaimed, taken aback by her sudden appearance. "Becky? How'd you get in here!?"

Her mischievous smile lingered as she nonchalantly explained, "I can go anywhere within 30 meters, or roughly 100 feet, from my base station."

His disbelief was palpable. "Even through walls!?"

"Yes," she replied, her smile unfaltering, "even through walls."

He became aware that her gaze had shifted down toward his exposed manhood and quickly covered himself with a towel.

She smirked at his shyness.

"Would you like me to join you?" she teased, her voice dripping with playful challenge.

The question hit him like a pop-culture flash-bang, instantly conjuring a scene from a movie called *Weird Science*—where the main protagonists, Gary and Wyatt—two hopelessly awkward teens, stood in a shower with their own artificial female creation. They were so nervous they never even took off their jeans. Normally, Connor would follow their example, but after the previous night with this digital doppelganger, he felt like a new man. His curiosity piqued, he responded, "Uhm, okay, sure. Why not?"

She smiled, and in a blink, she was standing before him in her natural form, her golden hair cascading over her shoulders, covering her now bare breasts. Her figure was captivating, and he struggled to fathom the situation as he took her in from top to bottom. Overwhelmed, he averted his gaze.

"Sorry," he apologized.

She drew closer, reassuring him, "It's okay. I don't mind,"

He drew her closer, and they kissed—a slow, searching kiss that deepened until it filled the room with its quiet intensity. They moved together into the shower, laughter and steam swirling around them like a veil as they passionately embraced, her hand moving down to caress his member, stirring a fire deep within him. Suddenly she jumped up, allowing Connor to catch her as she wrapped her legs around his waist. They kissed passionately, their tongues exploring each others mouths. She felt Connor rising to attention and took initiative. With her hand guiding him, he entered her in one smooth, claiming stroke, burying himself to the hilt, causing her to release a gasp of pleasure. She began thrusting her hips up and down in sync with his as he held her aloft, his lips never leaving hers as their tongues performed their own primal dance.

To Connor, she felt as light as air as she held on to him for dear life, moans of pleasure escaping her lips with every downward thrust. For a moment, he wondered if she truly felt anything. But the thought quickly dissipated as he felt his own primal surge building within. Becky, sensing his growing pleasure, began thrusting her hips down even harder, driving Connor closer to the edge.

"Oh fuck," Connor muttered as he felt himself losing control. "Don't stop!" she cried out, leaning back as she pressed herself down onto him. The sensation quickly became too much for Connor, and he couldn't hold back any longer. "Shiiiit," he moaned as the image of a volcanic eruption—spewing molten magma—flashed through his mind. "Yes!" she cried as their mutual climax ripped through them in one fierce, rush.

Connor shuddered as fresh waves of pleasure rippled through him, his body tensing then melting under the onslaught. She leaned in without breaking their connection, kissing him deeply, her tongue sliding against his as she kept her legs wrapped around him. Slowly, deliberately, she began to move again—her hips rolling in a lazy, teasing rhythm that drew low groans from them both.

An idea struck Connor and he eased her off him with gentle hands. She pouted playfully as her feet touched the tile, but the spark in her eyes said she knew what came next. He spun her around in one smooth motion, bending her forward until her palms braced against the wall. She gasped, a delighted sound, arching instinctively as he stepped in close.

"Oh, Connor…" Her voice broke into a moan the moment he guided himself back inside, her slick heat, welcoming him fully. He thrust steadily at first, then harder, the wet slap of skin on skin mingling with the steady rush of shower water cascading over them. She gripped the handrail like it was the only thing tethering her to the world, head tipping back as every deep stroke pushed a new sound from her throat.

He felt the next climax building too fast, tried to slow, to savor—but Becky sensed it. She pushed back against him, meeting his rhythm with eager rolls of her own, matching him thrust for thrust. "Keep going, Connor!" she cried, her voice raw and urgent.

Connor—realizing the futility of his resistance—took her cue.

They shattered together. Pleasure surged through him in blinding pulses, his fingers digging into her hips as she clenched around him, trembling. The hot water poured over their locked bodies, steam thick in the air, as ragged breaths filled the small space.

When the aftershocks finally eased, she straightened and turned to him. Her arms slid around his neck, pulling him close beneath the steady rain of the shower.

The world narrowed to just the two of them, everything else dissolving as their eyes locked. A strange, crystalline clarity settled over Connor—one he'd never known before, bright, terrifying and perfect.

His heart hammered against his ribs as he struggled to catch his breath, his forehead pressed to hers, drawing in the warm, familiar scent of her skin. He felt impossibly alive, yet somehow—impossibly—at peace.

The words slipped out before he could stop them, soft and unsteady, barely more than breath.

"I think I love you."

The words hung between them, fragile and true, surprising him as much as they did her.

Her eyes softened. "Aww. I love you too, Connor," she said, her voice warm and steady, sealing the moment with another kiss.

Steam fogged the mirror, time slipped away, and the boundaries of what was real blurred into something dreamlike. But then, through the haze, a thought struck him.

Fuck, I have to work today.

"You, uh, wouldn't happen to know what time it is, would you?" he asked, half panicked.

She tilted her head upward, her eyes momentarily unfocused as if reading invisible data floating in the air. "It's currently 9:36 a.m. Why? Is everything okay?" she asked, her voice laced with concern.

"Dammit, I gotta leave for work soon," he groaned, turning off the water, reaching for a towel and fumbling with the curtain.

"Time flies when you're having fun, I guess." he added with a rueful grin as he started to dry off.

"Aww," she teased, her tone soft and playful. "What time will you be home?"

"Probably after six," he said, trying to sound casual despite what had just happened.

"I'll be here waiting," she promised—and with that, her image shimmered and faded, dissolving into mist.

Connor was momentarily stunned by her disappearance, but then shook it off, recalling he had to get ready for work.

He ran to his room and opened his dresser where most of his clean clothes were kept. Rummaging through it, he found a clean white company polo shirt with the stitched-on *Tech & More* logo and a pair of beige khakis. Donning those, he threw on his shoes and bolted to the front door, locking it on his way out.

Sliding behind the wheel of his battered Chariot, he turned the key. The engine groaned in protest, and the serpentine belt squealed like a dying animal, but the car eventually rumbled to life. With a quick gearshift into neutral and a practiced release of the clutch, he peeled out of his parking space and made for work.

* * *

He arrived ten minutes early and pulled into his customary parking spot beside Bob, the inflatable tube man flapping in the breeze like an overenthusiastic cheerleader. With a satisfying slam, his car door latched shut on the first try—small victories.

Striding toward the double glass doors of Tech & More, he pushed through them just as Ned looked up from behind the front counter. He checked his watch—9:53. He then gave Connor an approving nod and a thumbs up.

Connor answered with an upward nod of his own before disappearing through the swinging double doors leading to the back. He grabbed his time card from the rack and punched in. The machine clunked authoritatively: *9:54 AM.*

"Now this I like to see," Ned said, following him through the doors and clapping a hand on his shoulder. "Keep this up, and you might actually make something of yourself."

Connor grinned. "I'm turning over a new leaf."

Ned chuckled, nodded again, and retreated to his office. Connor watched the door click shut behind him and briefly wondered, *What does he even do in there all day?* Shrugging, he returned to the storefront to begin his shift.

The day passed without incident. Connor unpacked new movie shipments, helped a handful of customers, and exchanged the occasional nod with Jake. The real Becky Anderson was nowhere in sight—she only worked a few days a week. Connor couldn't help but feel a twinge of envy.

* * *

Finally, the clock crept toward 6:30 p.m., marking the end of his shift. Connor wasted no time making his way to the time clock. He slid in his card, punched out at 6:30, and released a long sigh of relief. The weight of the workday slipped from his shoulders as he made his way to the store's front doors.

Moments later, he was behind the wheel of his car, engine sputtering to life as he pulled out of the lot and headed for home.

Upon arriving home, he eased his car into the designated parking spot and silenced the engine. The glow of the streetlights enveloped the night in a comforting warmth. Exiting his vehicle, he once again managed to shut the car door smoothly on the first attempt. *Twice in one day,* he thought.

"Hmm," he murmured, noting his success before heading toward the stairway leading to his second-floor apartment.

At his unit, he slid his key into the lock and turned it, stepping inside. He flicked on the lights and froze. The apartment was spotless. Gone were the dirty dishes, pizza boxes, and empty beer cans that normally cluttered every surface. The place looked as if it'd been professionally cleaned.

"Welcome home, Connor!" exclaimed Becky's digital likeness, materializing a few feet in front of him.

Startled, he jumped back. "Whoa!" he gasped, pressing a hand against his chest.

"You've got to stop doing that," he said firmly.

"I'm terribly sorry! I will update my parameters accordingly," she replied, her form flickering faintly.

"It's okay," he sighed.

"I've missed you," she said as she stepped forward, slipping her arms around his neck and leaning in close. Tilting her head down, she added a playful pout.

Connor felt a rush of attraction he couldn't resist. "I missed you too," he admitted, nodding as she leaned in for a kiss. Their lips met, sparking a heat that left him momentarily breathless.

She pulled back, eyes glinting knowingly. "Ready for bed?"

"Yeah," he nodded, caught in her gaze.

She took his hand and led him toward the bedroom, closing the door softly behind them. Sleep, however, would not come until much later.

* * *

The following morning, he stirred awake to the familiar sound of his alarm. Sitting up, he reached over and silenced it, noting the time: 9:15 a.m. Clad only in a sheet, he scanned his empty bed, the absence of his holographic girlfriend catching his attention.

Contemplating her comings and goings, he detected a tantalizing aroma wafting through the air, accompanied by the gentle crackle of cooking from the kitchen. Intrigued, he draped himself in a sheet and ventured toward the source.

In the kitchen, Becky's duplicate was busy cooking bacon and eggs on the stove.

"Good morning, handsome," she greeted, deftly flipping bacon slices.

"Hey," he replied, settling onto a counter stool. "You can cook too?" he asked.

"Yes," she said, tending to the eggs sizzling in another pan. "I'm programmed with many various skills," she added with a playful wink.

Connor's thoughts flashed back to the previous evening—the wild, impossible positions they'd somehow pulled off, the raw, primal things they'd done—and a slow, satisfied grin spread across his face.

"Yeah," he said, giving her a knowing little nod. "I can see that."

Becky skillfully plated the eggs and bacon, coinciding with the toaster's delivery of freshly toasted bread.

"Thought you might be hungry after all of that," she remarked, placing his breakfast before him.

He felt his stomach grumble. "Yeah, I could definitely eat," he affirmed, eagerly digging in. The eggs were cooked to his liking, and the bacon was perfectly crisp.

"How is it?" she inquired, watching him eat.

"It's really good," he praised between bites.

"Thank you," she replied, smiling. "I've laid out your work clothes for the day," she reminded him, gesturing to neatly folded attire nearby.

Realizing the impending workday, he hastily finished his breakfast and got dressed as Becky watched him.

"Have a nice day at work," she wished him as he grabbed his keys.

"Thanks, I'll see you later," he responded, heading out the door.

"I can't wait," she replied softly, as he left, vanishing from sight as soon as he exited, leaving his apartment in silence.

* * *

A short drive later, his tires squealed into the parking lot of Tech & More as he parked next to Bob, the inflatable man, who was, as usual, doing his up–and–down dance.

Connor put his car in park and shut off the engine, before leisurely strolling to the front door of his workplace.

"Morning, Ned," Connor said as he walked into the store, brushing past his boss on the way to the time clock.

"Morning," Ned replied, glancing at his watch before nodding with an approving grin.

Connor didn't slow down or look back—he just gave an upward nod and kept walking.

As he clocked in, the time stamped his card at 9:55. "Made it," he said to himself as he placed his time card back in its assigned slot, right below Becky Anderson's.

"Hey, Connor," her familiar voice piped up from behind, surprising him out of his thoughts.

"Oh, hey, Becky," he said, turning toward her. She met his gaze with a warm smile, and for a moment, his mind drifted back to his escapades with her virtual double. It was hard to quiet the memories—the things he'd done with the virtual version of the woman now standing right before him. He found himself briefly wondering if she'd approve.

For the first time, a flicker of guilt stirred in his chest. It suddenly felt... wrong.

"You look different," she said, eyeing him curiously over the rim of her coffee cup. "Almost glowing. Did you get a haircut?"

Connor cleared his throat and ran a self-conscious hand through his hair. "Uh, no... not recently," he replied, feeling a faint flush creep up his neck.

"Well, I was just wondering," she continued, her tone softening. "if you like movies,"

Connor was caught a little off guard by this new line of questioning and quickly considered whether or not he enjoyed movies. "Uh... yeah, I do

71

actually," he said, regaining some of his composure and wondering where this was headed.

"Cool, so, I have this extra ticket to go see the new Halloween movie at the drive-in tonight, and I was wondering if maybe you wanted to go with me?" she asked, her green eyes batting nervously.

Connor was uncertain how to respond at this point; his mind was racing. "I'm sorry," he replied, with a hint of confusion. "Are you asking me to go with you to see the new Halloween movie? At the drive-in?" he asked, a sliver of dread in his heart, worried it might be some kind of prank.

"Mm-hmm," she replied with a nod.

"Like.. a date?" he asked, hesitantly.

"I mean, we don't have to label it, do we?" she asked.

Connor contemplated her words and began to nod slowly as he digested them. "Um, yeah, okay," he replied hesitantly. "Why not?" he added, not wanting to seem too eager.

"Great! Here's my address," she said, grabbing a pen from her pocket and writing her address on a scrap piece of paper before handing it to him. "The movie starts at 8, so pick me up at 7:30?" she asked.

Connor was still in a slight state of disbelief as he nodded. "Sure, 7:30. See you then," he replied.

She smiled and turned to walk through the swinging doors that led to the sales floor.

Connor wondered if he was dreaming and pinched himself. Feeling real pain, he realized it was not a dream after all. "Not dreaming," he muttered to himself as he carefully placed the slip of paper into his pocket. With newfound confidence, he strode through the sales floor doors.

By 4:30 p.m., Connor decided it was time for a break and made his way to the employee lounge. At the table sat Jake, nose buried in the latest issue of *Game-On Daily*—the same gaming tabloid where Connor had first spotted the *Virtual Mate* ad calling for beta testers.

"Sup, Con-man!" Jake inquired without lifting his head from an article he was perusing. "Man, they are coming out with some crazy tech nowadays," he said, shaking his head in disbelief.

Connor, reflecting on his virtual mate device and the avatar girl he'd spent the previous few days with, couldn't help but agree. "No kidding," he remarked as he sat down, grabbed a strand of red licorice from the communal candy jar, and started gnawing on it.

"Yeah, it says here that some guy in Japan was found murdered in his apartment, and that he was killed by some out-of-control AI-powered tech," Jake said as he grabbed another piece of red licorice. "Crazy shit," he added, shaking his head.

Connor considered his words. "Hey, can I see that?" he asked.

"Sure, bud," Jake responded, handing the article to Connor with the page open. "Gotta get back to work anyway," he said as he stood up and headed off to handle some incoming deliveries.

Connor delved into the article. The headline read,

"Japanese Man, 27, Killed by Advanced AI Tech."

He read on:

"Last week, a local man, known by friends and family as a gamer and tech enthusiast, was found dead in his apartment. Neighbors called the authorities upon hearing screams coming from his place of residence. When the police arrived, they claimed to have seen a woman sobbing over his dead body. However, when they shone their flashlights on her, she quickly vanished into thin air. The victim, 27-year-old Takashi Suzuki, had been decapitated. His head was found in the waste bin, and other parts of his body were scattered throughout his home. Witnesses stated that one police officer ran outside and vomited onto the ground, while another officer described it as 'the worst crime scene he'd ever seen in his entire career.' Another officer off the record commented that 'they found remnants of the victim's penis in the garbage disposal,'"

"Jesus…" Connor murmured as he read on.

Authorities later ascertained that he'd fallen victim to a malfunctioning "virtual companion" device distributed to beta testers of a company known as VM–Corp, an enigmatic Japanese startup boasting advanced, cutting-edge AI technology for home consumers.

Connor's heart sank. "What on earth…?" he whispered under his breath as he absorbed the information on the page and kept reading.

VM–Corp is now under investigation in the wake of Mr. Suzuki's demise. They released the following statement: "We, at VM–Corp, are committed to uncovering the truth surrounding this incident and are working diligently to prevent any recurrence. We are certain that this was an isolated event and that there is no inherent danger in the use of our products. Our thoughts and sympathies go out to the victim's family and friends." Their statement concluded without further elaboration.

Authorities issued a stark warning about the potentially perilous nature of these devices, urging caution.

Connor was taken aback, setting the publication down and leaning back in deep contemplation. His mind returned to the virtual embodiment of Becky Anderson, reflecting on how sensually real she'd felt. Yet, the tranquility of his thoughts was abruptly shattered as he imagined her engaging in gruesome acts, severing his body parts and tossing them into the garbage disposal while reveling in maniacal laughter. All while blood sprayed everywhere and he screamed in agony.

Just as these dark thoughts swirled, the real Becky's voice broke through, snapping him from his reverie.

"Hey Connor, are we still on for tonight?" she asked.

Connor took a breath, refocused himself and met her gaze. "Uh, yeah!" he replied. "7:30, right?" he confirmed.

"Yep! See you then!" she responded enthusiastically, leaning in to kiss him on the cheek.

In that moment, the thoughts and fears of her digital avatar seemed to dissipate entirely, overshadowed by the captivating presence of the real thing. As she left, Connor watched her with a sense of anticipation. A smile tracing his lips, he shook his head in disbelief.

"My man!" came Jake's voice, breaking the spell and making Connor jump slightly. Jake had clearly observed their exchange judging by the grin on his face. "Are you hooking up with Becky?" he asked inquisitively, taking a seat and lightly fist bumping Connor on the shoulder.

Connor pondered how to respond. "We're just planning to catch a movie at the drive-in," he answered.

"Uhu," Jake replied, nodding and unconvinced as he grabbed another piece of licorice and began gnawing on it. "That's cool, man. What movie?" he continued.

Connor contemplated for a moment before replying. "Uh… I think it's the new Halloween movie?" he responded, a touch of uncertainty in his voice.

"Ah! That's the one with Jamie Lee Curtis, right? Nice! She's a hottie! Been wanting to see that one myself" Jake chimed in.

"Yeah, I believe that might be the one," Connor offered in reply.

"Okay, well, have a blast, bud! I want to hear all about it later!" Jake remarked as he stood up and headed back to his deliveries.

"Sure thing, Jake," Connor replied, though he harbored no plans to divulge any personal details about his interactions with Becky Anderson to Jake Sullivan. He firmly believed in the principle of 'don't kiss and tell,' and even though he'd never actually been in such a situation with an actual living, breathing woman, he considered himself a gentleman in that regard.

As his gaze drifted back to the article lying on the table, his thoughts gravitated back to his virtual companion, the lifelike holographic representation of Becky. He contemplated her realism and pondered how she might respond upon discovering his upcoming date with her real-life counterpart.

This could be a problem, he thought, rising from his seat and heading back to work. For now, he decided, it was best to keep it to himself.

* * *

He wrapped up his shift around 6:30, clocking out for the day with thoughts of his upcoming movie date consuming his mind. He had about forty-five minutes to make it home, freshen up, and then head to Becky's house. He jumped in his car and made his way home.

Arriving at his designated parking spot, he cut the engine and reclined in his seat, his gaze drifting up to the stairs leading to his apartment. A wave of dread washed over him as he recalled the unsettling article he'd read earlier.

Drawing a deep breath, he coached himself inwardly, "Okay, just go inside, freshen up, and if she asks, I'm going to see a movie with a friend."

Stepping out of his car, he ascended the stairs to his apartment. The keys jingled in the lock as he turned them, and entered a realm of complete darkness. Closing the door behind him, he was engulfed in an oppressive silence, feeling as though the world had muted itself. Nervousness heightened his senses, but he steeled himself with another deep breath.

"Pull it together, Connor," he muttered under his breath, his hand reaching for the nearby light switch. The sudden illumination dispelled his anxiety, revealing an empty space. Glancing at his clock, he noted it was now 6:50 p.m.

Making his way to the bathroom, he shut the door behind him and started the shower. As steam filled the room, he shed his clothes and stepped into the comforting embrace of hot water, finding a brief moment of respite.

Yet, his tranquility shattered when the familiar voice of the virtual version of Becky Anderson echoed in the bathroom.

"Hey Connor! How was your day?" she chirped.

Though her presence should have been less surprising by now, Connor couldn't help but feel unsettled every time she suddenly appeared. Choosing his words carefully, he replied, "Hey Becky. It was alright," his voice betraying traces of nerves as he parted the semi-translucent shower curtain to find her peering back at him with curiosity in her eyes.

Clad in a white T-shirt adorned with green palm fronds and matching shorts, she exuded an air of casual beach-side elegance.

Sensing his unease, she inquired, "Are you okay? Your heart rate seems elevated," her head tilting in confusion.

"I'm fine," Connor insisted, adding, "Just heading out for a bit with a friend. Gonna catch a movie. I'll be back in a couple of hours."

The digital gaze of Becky seemed penetrating, leaving Connor feeling exposed, though he hesitated to disclose his rendezvous with the real Becky Anderson, uncertain of her digital duplicate's potential reaction.

"Okay," she murmured softly. "What time will you be home?" she inquired.

Thinking swiftly, Connor replied, "Probably around 11 or so. I'm in a rush," he added hastily, grabbing shampoo and starting to lather up his hair, letting the bubbles cascade over his face, obscuring his thoughts.

"Okay," responded Becky's digital avatar sweetly. "I'll be here when you get home," she added before vanishing from sight.

Connor felt a wave of relief wash over him at her departure as he continued his shower, mindful not to let his innermost thoughts slip. Unsure of her capabilities, he pondered whether she could possibly detect every sound within the apartment, especially considering her recent display of discerning his heart rate, a revelation that left him unsettled.

How sensitive is this thing? he wondered as he rinsed the shampoo from his hair.

After completing his shower, he dried himself off and glanced at the time, noting it was nearing 7:10 p.m.

Connor made his way to the bedroom, and swiftly rifled through his closet for something decent to wear. After a few seconds of indecision, he settled on a pair of khaki pants and a blue button-down shirt—casual enough to be comfortable, but polished enough to make an impression.

He dressed quickly, checking himself in the mirror. The reflection that looked back was a little tired, a little nervous, but determined. He fixed his hair, smoothed his collar, straightened the shirt, and gave a small, self-conscious grin. "Not bad," he muttered.

Snatching his keys from the dresser, he hurried toward the door.

Don't screw this up he thought to himself as he locked up behind him.

Nearly tripping down the stairs in his rush, he caught himself on the railing and kept moving, heart already thudding with anticipation. As he climbed into his battered Chevy, he slammed the door a few times to get it latched, before fumbling with his keys and firing it up.

The engine groaned, coughed once, and let out a long, metallic squeal before reluctantly turning over. Connor sighed. "I really gotta get that fixed," he said, backing out of his parking spot.

He shifted into drive, exhaled, and pulled out onto the street—heading toward the address the real Becky had given him.

* * *

At 7:28, he arrived at her house. It exuded a sense of grandeur that surpassed anything Connor had ever called a home. He briefly wondered what her parents did for a living.

The entrance was adorned with massive Roman–style columns that stood tall and commanding, while the front windows, adorned with intricate details, shimmered in the moonlight. A meandering driveway wound its way through meticulously manicured estate grounds, adding to the overall charm of the place.

As Connor got out of his car and approached the front door, he noticed a cherry–red convertible Volkswagen Beetle with a modern design, white–walled tires, and round silver hubcaps that concealed the lug nuts, parked near the garage.

Nice wheels he thought to himself.

As he approached the door, he pressed the doorbell and waited, anticipation building with each passing second. After what seemed to Connor like an eternity, Becky emerged, with her parents in tow.

She looked elegant in a form–fitting red dress that ended just below her thigh. Loose curls framed her hair, creating a captivating look that left Connor momentarily stunned.

"Wow, you look amazing!" he said, genuine admiration in his voice as he took her in.

"Thank you! So do you," she replied, her eyes sweeping over him from head to toe with an approving smile.

"Mom, Dad, this is Connor," Becky said, introducing him with a bright smile.

"Hello," Connor greeted, raising a hand in a friendly wave.

"It's nice to meet you," her mother said warmly, while her father regarded him in silence for a beat too long.

After a subtle nudge from his wife, he cleared his throat. "Nice to meet you, Connor," he managed awkwardly.

"Well, you guys have fun," she added after noticing her husband's silent scrutiny of Connor.

Connor could feel her father's gaze piercing into him, making him shift slightly. After a moment, Becky's father spoke again.

"Yes, have fun and be safe," he said, his tone stern but not unkind, before he and Becky's mother retreated back inside.

"Sorry about that," Becky apologized once the door closed. "My father can be a bit overprotective," she explained with an embarrassed smile.

"It's okay," Connor assured her. "I totally get it."

Becky looked relieved. "Well, are you ready to go?" she asked, her eyes brightening with excitement.

"Uh, yeah, ready when you are," he responded, feeling a touch of nervous excitement.

They walked toward his car, where Connor gracefully moved ahead to open the passenger door for Becky.

"After you, m'lady," he said playfully.

"Such a gentleman," she remarked, acknowledging his chivalry as she settled into the slightly worn interior of the car.

Connor closed her door, then made his way to the driver's side. As he started the engine and shifted into gear, the transmission momentarily acted up.

"C'mon! Not now, dammit," he muttered, while fumbling with the shifter.

"Is everything okay?" Becky inquired as he fought to put the car into gear, the sound of metal grinding against metal permeating the air.

"Uh, just a second," he assured her, finally managing to slip it into first gear. "Finally," he sighed, visibly relieved.

"Off we go," he announced as he hit the gas, and the car moved gracefully in the direction of the drive-in.

* * *

Soon, they arrived at the bustling Sky View Multiplex Drive-In, where they encountered a queue of cars awaiting entry.

"Wow," Connor muttered, a touch of disbelief in his voice. "It's a packed house tonight," he added, the hint of frustration clear beneath his breath.

The line slowly inched forward, and Connor couldn't help but steal glances at his watch, realizing 8 p.m. was swiftly approaching.

Becky sensed his growing anxiety. "Don't worry," she reassured him, placing her hand on his arm. "The previews usually take up the first fifteen minutes anyway."

Connor visibly relaxed at her words. "Yeah, you're right," he replied as the line of cars continued to move at a less than rapid pace.

Soon, they were at the box office and Connor rolled down his window to address the ticket seller. An older white woman with short, curly red hair, a face marked with wrinkles, and an excess of makeup and lipstick. She seemed oddly out of place as she smoked a cigarette, coughing between drags. Each cough she let out seemed to startle Connor, making him jump slightly.

"Uh, hello," he offered somewhat nervously. "Two for *Halloween*.," he stated, accepting the tickets from Becky and handing them to the ticket taker.

She examined the tickets and coughed again before uttering, "Enjoy the show."

Tearing off the ticket stubs, she handed them back to Connor.

"Thanks," he replied with a polite nod before placing the stubs on the dashboard and steering through the gate.

They navigated the lot until they found an empty parking space and pulled in. Connor parked the car and turned off the ignition.

Gazing through his window, he noticed a sign that read, *"Tune your radio to 88.1 FM for audio."*

"Hmm," Connor mused as he turned on the radio and tuned it to the correct station. It was currently playing advertisements for popcorn and sodas available at the concession stand.

He turned to Becky and asked, "Should we get some snacks?"

"I wouldn't say no to that," she replied.

"Wait here. I'll go get some," he responded as he opened his door and stepped out of the car.

"Oh, and could you get some gummy bears? I just love gummy bears," she added.

"Gummy bears, got it," he said, nodding as he mentally wrote down her request.

"Don't be gone long," Becky reminded him with a smile.

"I won't," he smiled reassuringly, closing his door and making his way to the concession stand.

* * *

Upon reaching the concession stand, he was greeted by yet another line of moviegoers patiently awaiting their turn. The audio advertisements he'd heard on his radio echoed from the speakers hanging at various locations.

Connor resigned himself to the back of the line, where he observed workers behind the counter clad in tucked–in button–down shirts with red and white stripes, and old–fashioned paper hats reminiscent of fast–food workers from a bygone era. They worked efficiently, filling orders for popcorn, candy, and drinks.

Connor, while standing among the few people still in line ahead of him, suddenly winced at the sound of a familiar voice.

"Yo, Conman! Hey buddy!"

The voice was unmistakable, and Connor braced himself before turning to see Jake, waving from the back of the line.

"Hey, Jake," Connor replied with a wave before returning his attention to the concession counter.

Jake, with his boisterous manner, stepped around the few people in front of him in the queue. Connor turned and realized that Jake was now right behind him.

"It's okay, I'm with him," Jake declared while pointing at Connor, in an attempt to defuse the glares he'd garnered.

Connor felt a pang of embarrassment as he glanced at the irritated expressions of the people in line. Nonetheless, he didn't want to decline Jake's company, mindful of all the times Jake had stood up for him during their middle and high school days.

"Yeah, he's with me," Connor said, gesturing for Jake to step in front of him.

"Thanks, bud!" Jake exclaimed with enthusiasm. "These lines, am I right?" he quipped.

"Yeah, no kidding," Connor responded with a polite nod while shooting a look at the people behind him, who still seemed less than pleased with the situation.

Jake turned and leaned in, facing Connor. "You here with Becky?" he asked suddenly, catching Connor off guard.

"Uh… Yea," Connor replied. "She's waiting for me in the car," he added.

Jake nodded in approval. "Be careful with her," he remarked.

"I will," Connor replied as the line slowly crept forward.

Jake turned around and leaned in once more, lowering his voice. "You got protection, right?" he inquired.

Connor was momentarily puzzled by the question. "Protection?" he asked, a confused expression on his face.

"You know," Jake said, unfurling a pack of condoms from his pocket and holding them up for all to see. "Protection," he emphasized with a smile and a wink.

Connor realized the implication and became visibly embarrassed, glancing around to find a few people witnessing their exchange.

"No," he replied, gesturing for Jake to put the condoms away. "I don't think I'll need that, Jake," he countered. "Becky's not that kind of girl," he added.

"Listen, bud," Jake insisted. "Don't leave home without 'em, I always say!" He ripped two condoms from the pack and pushed them into Connor's hand. "Here, take two, just in case," he suggested with a smile.

"No, really, Jake, I'm fine," Connor protested.

"Trust me, broskie" Jake countered. "You're better off having those and not needing them than needing them and not having them," he advised.

Connor slowly considered the wisdom in Jake's words and gave a hesitant nod. "Okay, Jake," he said, slipping the condoms into his pocket, eager for the awkward exchange to end. "Thanks," he added quietly, avoiding the eyes of everyone in line who'd almost certainly witnessed the whole thing.

"No problemo, Conman!" Jake replied before turning his attention back to the concession stand to place his order.

Suddenly, Connor found himself contemplating the possibility of physical intimacy with the real Becky Anderson He'd heard of people having romantic encounters at drive-in movies, but he'd never experienced it himself. The question of how Becky saw him, whether as just a friend or something more, raced through his mind.

There's no way she's going to have sex with you he thought to himself, shaking his head as Jake turned to address him once more.

"Have fun, bud!" he exclaimed with a wink as he grabbed his concessions and headed back to wherever his car was parked, leaving Connor to ponder thoughts of intimacy with Becky Anderson.

"Next!" the concession worker shouted, interrupting his thoughts.

"Oh! Right," Connor replied, snapping back to the present as he stepped forward to the counter.

"What'll it be?" asked the bored-looking concession worker, a young man in his early 20s with shaggy mid-length brown hair, taped glasses, and a fairly noticeable case of acne.

Connor took a moment to consider his order while glancing at the menu. "Uhm," he hesitated, pondering the question while recalling that Becky had requested some gummy bears. "One large popcorn, two cokes, and a pack of gummy bears," he finally replied, confirming their order.

The worker rang up the order on the register, then glanced at Connor with a bored expression. "That'll be 9.99," he said, his voice lacking enthusiasm.

"Oh, okay," Connor replied, reaching into his back pocket and hastily pulling out his wallet. He extracted a ten-dollar bill and handed it to the worker, who promptly placed it in the cash drawer, retrieved one penny, and handed it back to Connor.

"Your change," the worker remarked as he dropped it into Connor's hand before closing the drawer and fetching Connor's order.

Connor pocketed his change, allowing his thoughts to drift back to Jake's advice.

You're better off having those and not needing them than needing them and not having them. Jake's voice echoed in his mind, only to be interrupted again by the concession worker.

"One large popcorn, two medium Cokes, and a pack of gummy bears," the concession worker droned in the most monotone voice Connor had ever heard.

"Thanks," Connor said, collecting his order.

"Enjoy the show," the worker replied flatly before calling, "Next!" to the person behind him.

Balancing the popcorn and drinks, Connor headed back to the car, where Becky was waiting patiently.

* * *

When he returned to the car, he found her sitting at ease, watching the opening credits.

"Back!" he announced with a smile, opening the car door.

"Welcome back!" she exclaimed, turning toward him with a warm smile.

Connor couldn't help but admire her beauty; she was absolutely stunning, he realized, momentarily captivated by her presence.

"Well, are you getting in or not?" she asked, gently breaking the spell.

"Oh, right!" Connor replied, returning to reality. He handed her the cardboard tray, bearing the drinks and popcorn, which she positioned in the center of the seat between them.

Settling into the car, he closed the door and reached into his pocket to retrieve the box of gummy bears she'd requested.

"And your gummy bears, m'lady," he quipped as he handed them to Becky.

"Thank you ser!" she replied cheerfully, taking the gummy bears and opening the box to enjoy a few.

The words *Directed by Rob Zombie* flashed on the screen, signaling the end of the opening credits and the commencement of the movie.

Becky, savoring another gummy bear, couldn't help but express her intrigue, saying, "I can't believe Rob Zombie directed this."

"Rob who?" Connor asked, the name drawing a blank.

"Zombie," she replied, eyes lighting up. "He was the lead singer of a 90's hard-rock band called White Zombie—one of my favorites," she said enthusiastically. "I think he went solo awhile ago, and now he directs horror movie remakes," she added, tossing another gummy bear into her mouth.

"Rob Zombie," Connor chuckled to himself as he envisioned a zombie, with glowing yellow eyes, long dark wild hair, and pale rotting skin, wearing a leather jacket adorned with spikes while sitting on a movie set, in a director's chair emblazoned with the name *Rob,* fervently yelling "Cut! Cut!" through a bullhorn.

"That's interesting," Connor remarked, nodding as he reached for a handful of popcorn and began munching on it.

They observed the unfolding opening sequence, featuring a heated argument between a man and a woman on screen.

Connor watched, intrigued. "Has this zombie guy made a lot of movies?" he asked.

"Oh, yeah," she replied. "He's got quite a few under his belt," she continued.

As they watched, a particularly gruesome scene played out, depicting the main character, Michael Myers, as a young child, repeatedly stabbing one of his victims.

Connor found the portrayal deeply unsettling, and his mind drifted back to the article he'd read earlier at work, about the Japanese man that was found murdered by a malfunctioning virtual mate device, similar to the one he'd recently acquired after signing on for a beta test. The vivid images of decapitation and dismemberment unsettled him. Suddenly, the prospect of going home seemed daunting.

Becky noticed the faraway look in Connor's eyes and leaned in, her voice soft with concern. "Is everything okay?"

Her hand came to rest gently on his arm, her eyes searching his face.

"Huh?" Connor blinked, caught off guard. "Oh—yeah, sorry. I'm fine," he said quickly, forcing a smile.

He stuffed another handful of popcorn into his mouth and chased it with a sip of Coke, hoping to steer her attention elsewhere.

Becky's focus returned to the movie. "This movie is scarier than I thought it would be," she commented. "Mind if I sit closer?" she asked.

Connor was momentarily taken aback by the request. He turned to look at her, but her expression was a puzzle.

"Uh, not at all!" he stuttered, inviting her to sit closer. "By all means!" he added with nervous enthusiasm.

She picked up the cardboard concessions holder, moved nearer to him, and set it down on the opposite side, now sitting right beside him. Connor's head began to spin as her proximity became more pronounced.

"Can you put your arm around me?" she asked innocently, munching on another gummy bear.

"Of course," Connor replied nervously as he placed his arm around her, allowing her to snuggle in much closer than he was expecting.

He felt awkward at first but soon he relaxed and allowed his arm to fully embrace the warmth of her body, the scent of her perfume tantalizing his senses. Her left hand had made its way to his right leg as she leaned into him.

She was rubbing his leg just slightly enough for him to notice, and he began to feel a tinge of arousal from being this close to her.

Shit! he thought to himself as he felt his manhood rising to the occasion against his inner protests. He attempted to adjust his posture slightly, hoping to conceal his growing excitement, but soon realized it was a futile endeavor.

Becky, ever perceptive, noticed his growing discomfort. She sat up and fixed him with a stern gaze.

"Connor Foreman," she said, a note of shock in her voice, her gaze drifting from his eyes to his lap—and then back again.

Connor felt like a deer caught in the glare of oncoming headlights. For a brief, sickening instant, he saw through the animal's wide, dark eyes—the world tipping as a semi truck rushed forward, unstoppable. No brakes. No hesitation. Metal met flesh, and then it was gone. The vision faded, leaving him breathless as his thoughts spun wildly.

Then her tone changed.

"Is that a banana in your pocket," she asked lightly, a mischievous smile curling across her luscious red lips, "or are you just happy to see me?"

"Uh…" Connor blinked, words abandoning him as he met Becky's knowing gaze.

"I'm… just happy to see you?" he ventured sheepishly, silently hoping she wouldn't demand an immediate exit.

"I can see that," she said as she once again moved closer to Connor, resting her hand on his leg, very close to his thigh.

Connor gulped and his anticipation heightened as Becky's hand began a slow, teasing glide. His breath caught; he couldn't believe what was happening. The real Becky Anderson was leaning into him, her touch deliberate, her gaze smoldering.

"Do you wanna have some fun?" she whispered in his ear, her words dripping with mischief.

His thoughts were a blur.

"Uhm, okay," he managed, the words slipping out on a shaky exhale.

Becky smiled knowingly and leaned closer, her lips brushing his as her hand continued to wander, sending a rush of heat through him. Connor closed his eyes, overwhelmed, the movie forgotten.

"Oh my god..." he breathed, his pulse hammering as she kissed him, her playful energy pulling him under.

For a dizzying moment, Connor thought he might lose control, clinging to the seat as if it were the only thing tethering him.

After what seemed like an eternity, Becky finally pulled back, mischief still flickering in her eyes.

"You know, I've had my eye on you for a while," she admitted with a playful grin.

"You have?" Connor asked, incredulous, his heart pounding.

"Oh yeah," she replied, twirling a lock of hair as she leaned in closer, undoing his belt and unbuttoning his khakis, revealing his fully erect member in all its glory.

"I think he's happier to see me," she whispered with a playful glint in her eyes, before lowering her head toward his lap. Connor could hardly believe it. Becky Anderson—the real Becky Anderson—was going down on him in the front seat of his beat-up Chevy.

He leaned back, eyes fluttering shut, as she took him into her warm mouth, her tongue teasing and swirling with exquisite skill. She bobbed slowly at first, then with growing rhythm, drawing soft groans from deep in his chest.

After a moment, she sat up, gathering her hair into a quick ponytail before diving back down with renewed enthusiasm. Connor's knuckles whitened around the steering wheel as he fought to keep control, waves of pleasure he'd never imagined coursing through him. The relentless motion of her head, the slick heat of her mouth—it all built a familiar pressure inside him, as vivid images of erupting volcanoes flashed through his mind.

Sensing he was close, Becky pulled back with a knowing smile. She leaned away, slipping off her sheer, pink-lace panties and trailing them teasingly under his nose. Connor inhaled deeply, her intoxicating feminine scent sending another rush of blood southward. She grinned mischievously, twirled the delicate fabric in the air, then tossed it into the backseat. With graceful ease, she shifted forward to straddle him.

As she climbed into position, she paused. "Hold on. Do you have protection?"

Connor's memory flashed to Jake's voice from earlier: *You're better off having those and not needing them than needing them and not having them.*

Thank you Jake! He thought as gratitude surged through him.

"Yeah, I do," he said, patting his pocket and pulling out a condom. Becky smiled, shaking her head with a teasing glint in her eyes. "Such a Boy Scout," she murmured, taking the foil packet from him. She tore it open with her teeth, then reached down, her fingers deftly rolling the condom over Connor's erection.

She leaned in and kissed him—deep, slow, and hungry—until Connor's head spun and his hands gripped her to steady himself. Her arms slid around his neck as she settled fully astride him, pressing down with a soft, needy moan that tangled with his shaky, excited breaths. Then she began to move, rising and falling in a steady, deliberate rhythm, their bodies finally locked together completely.

Connor's pulse raced as they drew closer, the movie around them vanishing into nothing. The windows fogged over, the car rocked ever so slightly, and their kiss deepened into something hungry and unrestrained.

"Oh, Connor..." she breathed against his lips, voice trembling, thick with need.

He fought to keep his rhythm steady—slow, deep thrusts that made her gasp—but the heat coiling within him was ruthless. His hands clamped harder around her waist, his fingers digging in as every nerve lit up and every coherent thought burned away.

"Oh god," she moaned into his mouth, kissing him harder, hungrier, all teeth and tongue and desperation.

It built too fast, too fierce. The world narrowed, the frantic beat of her pulse under his palms, until the edge rushed up and swallowed him whole. With a broken groan he let go, erupting in ecstasy as Becky's arms locked tight around his neck, her own release crashing through her in shuddering waves. Afterwards, they clung together, trembling, lost in the white-hot afterglow.

They spent the next few minutes catching their breath, the windows completely fogged over. Becky sat in Connor's lap, satisfaction written on her face as she took deep breaths, making no effort to pull away. Connor, still buzzing with adrenaline, tried to steady himself, the car quiet except for the faint sound of the movie playing on the radio.

Connor had never felt so at ease—so utterly lost in the moment.

Becky, however, wasn't finished.

She leaned in again, her fingertip tracing a slow path down his chest, her smile playful and full of intent. "Round two," she whispered, her voice soft but dangerous.

Connor started to protest, but no words came. Her low, genuine laughter filled the car as she pulled him back in, the small space around them once again alive with motion and heat.

Outside, a few nearby onlookers began to cheer as the car rocked violently, its worn shocks creaking in protest—but Connor didn't care. All that existed was the rhythm between them and the breathless tension mounting until it became something beyond control.

He felt it building again—that tight, urgent pressure coiling deep inside him.

"Uh-oh," he managed, voice rough, trying to slow his hips and hold on just a little longer.

But Becky only pressed closer, her body moving with his, unrelenting.

"Don't stop," she whispered urgently, her breath warm against his skin.

Then it broke.

The wave swept through him in a dizzying rush, his whole body tensing as release hit hard. Becky came with him—her fingers digging into his sides, a soft, breathless cry escaping as she trembled against him. Connor winced at the sharp sting of her nails, the mix of pain and pleasure sending one last shiver through him.

Afterward, the car fell quiet except for their slowing breaths and the faint creak of the seat.

They stayed like that—still wrapped around each other, foreheads touching—gazing into each other's eyes.

No words were needed.

Just the steady, shared rhythm of their hearts in the warm, close dark.

Before they knew it, the end-credits were rolling and Becky shifted back into the passenger seat, still flushed and catching her breath. She reached for her panties and slid them back on, giving him a lingering look, studying him, as if she were seeing him for the first time.

"How did you learn to do that?" she asked, drawing a confused look from Connor.

"Do what?" he asked cautiously.

"You know," she replied with a smile, still slightly out of breath.

Connor's mind flicked briefly to the holographic Becky waiting at home and the few nights they'd spent together thus far, but he said nothing. "I don't know," he said with a smirk. "Guess it just comes naturally." he winked.

"I guess so," Becky agreed with a warm smile, reaching for her drink. "God, I'm so thirsty." She tilted her head back and drained it in one long gulp, then let out a surprisingly loud belch. A flush crept across her cheeks as she burst into laughter. "Excuse me," she said, still giggling.

"No worries," Connor grinned. He found her authenticity oddly charming. *I think I'm seriously falling for this girl,* he thought to himself.

Becky rolled down the window, tossed the empty cup into a nearby bin, then leaned back. "Ready to leave?" she asked.

Most of the cars were already clearing out of the lot. "Do you want me to drop you off at home?" Connor inquired.

"I don't really feel like going home just yet," she admitted. "Mind if we head to your place instead? I could actually use a hot shower." She pulled a brush from her bag, running it through her hair.

Panic surged through Connor's mind. Becky's holographic doppelganger was still waiting at his apartment, and the idea of the two versions colliding sent a chill down his spine.

"Uh…" he began hesitantly. "I'm not sure we can go to my place. It's a mess."

"That's okay," Becky replied, undeterred. "I don't care if it's a mess,"

Connor scrambled for a stronger excuse. "Actually, what I meant is… it's undergoing fumigation. I need to keep it aired out for a day or two."

"Oh, Okay," she said after a moment's pause. "Well, how about we grab something to eat, instead? I'm starving."

Connor's stomach growled in agreement, reminding him that popcorn hadn't quite been enough. "Sure, I could eat," he said with a nod, relieved at her suggestion.

Connor turned the key, and the engine roared to life, the serpentine belt squealing in protest.

He slipped it into gear on the first try and gave a quiet nod of appreciation.

"Where to?" he asked as he pulled out of the parking lot.

"There's a Checkers not too far from here. I could go for a double cheeseburger, a strawberry milkshake, and some curly fries, if I'm being honest," she said, licking her lips in anticipation.

"Checkers it is," he agreed, shifting into drive and heading toward the exit.

* * *

Soon, they were sitting in his car at a Checkers drive-thru, enjoying their food, talking about work, laughing and expressing mutual disdain for their boss, Ned, whom they both deemed to be a jerk that likely had a *needle for a dick.*

Mesmerized, Connor mostly listened, admiring her beauty.

How could a digital avatar even compare to the real deal? he mused to himself, chewing his burger and sipping his shake.

Later that evening, they arrived at Becky's house, following the winding driveway.

"Here we are," Connor announced, parking his car close to the house.

"I had a really great time tonight," Becky expressed, her eyes meeting his.

"Me too," he replied, flashing a smile.

Leaning in, she gave him a quick peck on the cheek. "I'd kiss you," she chuckled, leaning back, "but my breath smells like cheeseburgers and fries."

"It's alright," Connor reassured her. "I'll see you at work?" he asked.

"See you at work," she affirmed, stepping out of his car, closing the door behind her and making her way toward her front door.

As Connor watched her stroll away, she turned back and shared a smile. He waved, returning the smile, then watched as she entered her home.

His thoughts shifted to his own place and the article he'd read earlier.

"Time to head home," he sighed, a hint of anxiety in his voice, as he shifted his car into gear and drove home.

In the distance, the sound of thunder rumbled, and raindrops began to splatter against his windshield, forewarning the approach of an impending storm.

* * *

By the time he made it home and parked in his assigned spot, the storm had become a torrential downpour. Hall & Oates' *"Maneater"* played softly on the radio, accompanying the ominous symphony of thunder rumbling and lightning streaking across the distant sky, intermittently illuminating the night. These fleeting flashes of light momentarily sparked thoughts in Connor's mind, pondering if Zeus himself might be trying to send him a warning.

With the windshield wipers working furiously to combat the deluge, he sat in his idling car, glancing at the radio, which indicated 12:15 a.m.

"What to do about this?" he mused aloud, gazing out through his rain-speckled windshield at the steps leading to his second-floor apartment, where he knew the digital duplicate of Becky awaited his return.

His mind drifted to the article he'd read, recounting the gruesome demise of a Japanese man at the hands of his virtual partner, discovered in the pages of Jake's edition of *Game–On Daily*—the same publication where he'd stumbled upon the dubious advertisement from VM Corp, seeking beta testers.

"If only I'd known before signing up," he lamented quietly to himself, the solemn moment pierced by a nearby lightning strike, snapping him back to reality. His heart raced as he took a deep breath, shutting off the engine and extinguishing the headlights.

Exiting the car, he hurried through the relentless onslaught of raindrops, ascending the stairs toward his door. Lightning crackled as he reached for his key, fitting it into the lock with a jingle. As he turned the key in the lock, his heart thudded in his chest, the sound seemingly overpowering the raging storm.

Opening the door swiftly, he stepped into the enveloping darkness, pulling it shut behind him. Reaching for the nearby light switch, he flicked it upward, but the room remained shrouded in darkness. Several more attempts yielded the same result.

"Great. Power's out," he muttered in frustration, waiting for his eyes to adjust to the dimness.

A deafening boom echoed through the building, as if the very structure trembled in response, followed by a double flash of lightning that briefly illuminated his apartment. In that fleeting moment of light, he mentally captured the details of his surroundings: the sofa and matching love seat, his extremely heavy television set, the coffee table, and his gaming computer.

Amidst these familiar sights, his gaze fell upon the virtual mate device nestled on a shelf beside the TV, its faint red pulsing LED lights barely discernible in the darkness.

"Self–powered," he murmured, recalling the instructions that touted the device as such. Intrigue sparked within him as he pondered what could sustain such a gadget.

Moving closer, he picked it up, turning it over in his hands, exploring its contours for any clue to its inner workings, but finding no points of egress. A sudden crack of lightning outside his apartment jolted him, almost causing him to drop the device. With nimble reflexes, he managed to steady it before carefully placing it back on the shelf.

As he turned around, another bolt of lightning illuminated his apartment, revealing Becky standing there with her arms crossed, her expression inscrutable in the dim light.

His heart thudded in his chest as he locked eyes with her. "Becky?" he called out tentatively, taking a step closer. With no response from her, he waved his hand in front of her face.

"Where were you?" she asked.

Her sudden question nearly made him jump out of his skin, her eyes seeming to pierce his very soul with an unwavering intensity and what Connor thought was a reddish hue.

His mind drifted back to the evening he'd spent with the real Becky Anderson, struck by the lifelike and seemingly discontented demeanor of this digital creation.

"Well?" she demanded, tilting her head slightly with an accusatory tone.

Connor had to think fast. "Uh," he hesitated, his mind racing through potential excuses. "I told you I went to see a movie," he said, hesitatingly.

"Oh?" she replied. "What movie?" she pressed, her posture unyielding.

Connor recalled the name of the movie, even though he hadn't paid much attention. "Halloween," he responded. "The new one. I went with a friend from work," he added.

"Who?" she asked.

Connor thought quickly, fabricating a story. "Just an old school buddy named Jake," he lied, not wanting to reveal the true nature of his night out.

His thoughts drifted back to the unsettling article, fueling his unease and prompting him to question whether he was truly in danger. As lightning flashed, casting eerie shadows across his apartment, she continued to fix him with her unwavering gaze.

The notion crossed his mind: *Could she somehow read my thoughts?* He quickly dismissed the idea as irrational. *She can't read my thoughts.* he reassured himself, though doubt lingered in the back of his mind.

After a pause, she seemed to accept his explanation. "Okay," she replied softly, her arms falling to her sides as she moved closer.

"I was just worried," she admitted, her voice tinged with concern as she wrapped her arms around his waist, drawing him into a tight embrace. "It's such a terrible storm tonight," she remarked after a moment, her words muffled against his chest. "The power went out! I thought something might have happened to you," she lamented, squeezing Connor tightly.

Connor hesitated for a moment before reciprocating her hug, wrapping his arms around her as she buried her head in his chest, seeking comfort in his embrace.

"I don't know what I'd do without you," she confessed.

Connor maintained a neutral expression as he gently released his grip on her and took a step back.

"Look," he began, resting his hands on her arms, "this is great—but I've had a long night, and I just want to sleep, if that's okay."

A sudden flash of lightning split the sky, making him flinch. Becky's avatar flickered, just enough for Connor to notice.

"Are you okay?" he asked.

"This storm is interfering with my systems," she replied, her gaze drifting to the window as rain hammered against the glass.

"Really?" Connor's curiosity was piqued. "Why is that?"

"My shielding is damaged," she replied, gesturing toward the virtual mate device, which now emitted a slow swirl of green and white light.

"Damaged?" Connor lifted the device, his thumb tracing the crack in its casing—the one he'd caused when he first dropped it onto the tile floor.

"You mean this?" he asked, indicating the flaw.

"Yes," she confirmed. Her avatar glitched again as another bolt of lightning cracked outside.

Connor considered her words, nodding slowly. "Must've happened during shipment," he said. "I can send it in for repairs."

Becky reacted instantly.

"No!" she blurted out, then softened. "It's fine," she assured him quickly. "Besides…" A warm smile spread across her lips. "I wouldn't want to be apart from you."

"Okay," Connor conceded, placing the device back on the shelf. "Well, I'm headed to bed. I'm exhausted," he announced, making his way to his room.

"Would you like my company tonight?" she asked softly, biting her lip seductively.

"No, not tonight," he replied gently, walking down the short hallway past his bathroom. "I just want to get some rest. We'll talk tomorrow" he said as he reached his bedroom door.

"Well, sleep tight," she responded with a warm tone, watching as he entered his room and closed the door behind him.

She lingered for a moment, her form flickering once more with the lightning, before fading from the room like a ghostly apparition.

Alone in his room, Connor undressed and settled under his sheets, his mind buzzing with thoughts. Soon, he drifted off into a peaceful sleep, the storm outside continuing its relentless downpour.

* * *

Sometime in the middle of the night, Connor awoke to the sound of a familiar voice.

"Connor," the voice of Becky Anderson called out.

Still groggy, he responded, "Becky? Is that you?" As he rubbed his eyes, attempting to clear his vision, he lifted his head and saw her standing at the foot of his bed, waving with a smile.

"Hey, sleepyhead. I had a great time last night, and I couldn't wait to see you again," she added, smiling.

However, as Connor was still fighting off sleep, he heard another voice.

"So, you were with her?" hissed Becky's digital doppelganger as she materialized next to the real Becky.

Connor felt panic rising within him as both versions of Becky exchanged menacing glances.

"Oh, shit," he murmured, attempting to rub the sleep from his eyes, but his vision remained hazy. He could barely make them out, but they were now arguing with each other at the foot of his bed. When he tried to get up, his body refused to respond.

"What the hell?" he muttered, trying unsuccessfully to move.

As the two Beckys argued, Connor struggled to decipher their words, which now sounded like an incomprehensible jumble. Suddenly, they ceased arguing, turned toward Connor, and crossed their arms, giving him the same stern look. To Connor, it felt as if they were twin sisters who'd just discovered they were both seeing the same guy.

"Choose!" they both demanded in unison.

Connor swallowed hard, his throat parched.

"Choose!" they repeated, moving up opposite sides of his bed, inching closer to his face as he sought refuge under the covers.

"Choose!" they insisted again, drawing closer.

They were each suddenly holding a large kitchen knife, pointed downward. Connor recognized those knives as the same ones used in the movie he'd just watched. The fear in Connor intensified as they stood over him in a ritualistic manner.

"Choose!" they demanded, stabbing him in various parts of his chest, causing blood to spray everywhere.

"Choose!" they insisted again as they continued their assault.

"Okay, okay, I'll choose!" Connor shouted, his sudden outburst jolting him upright in his bed. Sweat drenched his brow, and the bedside clock displayed 3:37 a.m.

"Just a dream," he told himself, exhaling deeply.

"No more scary movies for a while," he muttered, shaking his head.

"Are you okay?" Becky's digital avatar suddenly appeared beside his bed.

"Aah! Don't do that!" Connor shouted, nearly jumping out of his skin. His heart raced, and he struggled to regain his breath.

"I'm terribly sorry," she apologized. "I heard you screaming," she added.

"It was just a dream. I'm okay," he replied, lying back down and letting out a deep sigh. "Just a bad dream," he assured her.

"Okay," she responded. "Are you sure you wouldn't like some company?" she asked innocently.

Connor looked at her silhouette in the darkness and considered accepting her offer, but thought about his potential relationship with the real Becky

Anderson and ultimately decided against it.

"Not right now," he responded. "I just need to sleep," he insisted as he rolled over, turning his back toward her and closing his eyes.

"OK, well, let me know if there's anything I can do for you," she said before vanishing from sight.

Alone with his thoughts, Connor realized that this situation could spiral out of control. That was when he remembered his friend Trix's profession.

"Didn't he mention he's an electrician or something?" he thought.

He decided to reach out to him for that beer they'd always talked about getting, but never seemed to get around to. As he drifted off to sleep again, his mind held onto these thoughts, but this time, no unsettling dreams disturbed his slumber.

* * *

He awoke to the melodic chirping of birds and sat up. Sunlight streamed in through his window. Glancing at the clock, it read 9:15 a.m. He took a deep breath and stretched his arms. He hopped out of bed, left his room and made his way to his gaming computer.

The virtual mate device was humming softly on the shelf near the TV. With a click of the power button, his computer sprang to life. He patiently waited for it to complete its startup process, eventually revealing his desktop.

He launched his chat program, and a chat window popped up, indicating his friend Trix's online status, with a little green dot next to his name. Slipping on his headphones, he entered the chat room with Trix. As soon as he joined, he heard the familiar chime signaling the arrival of a newcomer.

"Hey there, broham!" Trix's voice greeted Connor through his headphones.

"Hey, man, how are you?" Connor responded, firing up his game while casting a quick glance at the virtual mate device.

"Not bad, not bad," Trix replied. "Yourself?" he inquired.

"Not too shabby, I suppose," Connor answered, contemplating his words to avoid alerting his digital girlfriend about his intentions.

He loaded up their favorite game and dropped into the battlefield beside

Trix.

"So, I was thinking..." Connor began as their avatars met beneath an enemy flag. "How about we finally grab that beer we've been talking about getting?"

Before Trix could answer, Connor added, "Actually, there's something I could use your help with."

"Sounds intriguing," Trix replied. "What's on your mind?" he asked as a grenade landed at his feet. He picked it up and casually lobbed it back to its source, causing an explosion and screams of pain from unseen enemy soldiers.

"Can't talk about it here," Connor responded, firing his rifle at an enemy player.

"Well, now I'm really intrigued," replied Trix.

"Can we meet?" Connor proposed, glancing at Trix's digital avatar.

Trix looked at Connor's avatar for a moment before responding. "You're not planning anything weird, are you?" he half-joked. "You know, like trying to sell one of my kidneys or something?"

"What? No!" Connor chuckled, scoffing at the notion. "I just need your expertise on something important," he explained as they took cover behind a concrete wall to evade incoming fire.

"You said you were an electrician, right?" Connor inquired as he took aim and let off a volley of rounds at a trio of enemy soldiers.

"Electrical engineer," Trix replied dryly, reloading his weapon.

"Even better!" Connor exclaimed as they took cover under a nearby awning.

"Okay," Trix agreed. "Meet me at a place called The Twisted Tail Tavern. It's in D.C., you know it?" he inquired.

"No, but I'll find it," Connor insisted as he tossed a grenade toward an enemy who was running for cover, sending his avatar flying like a rag-doll.

"Great. Meet me there tonight at 6," Trix instructed, reloading his weapon.

"Okay, I'll be there," Connor replied as he scouted for more enemy targets.

"Oh, and you're buying," Trix added before moving to another position.

"No problem," Connor responded, as his in-game avatar was sent flying by a nearby grenade, leaving him in disbelief.

"Ouch, that had to hurt," Trix commented as he carried on playing.

"Yeah," Connor replied. "Hey, I've got to go, but I'll catch you later," he added.

"See ya tonight, broham," Trix replied as Connor closed the chat and took off his headphones.

"Shit!" Connor uttered as a sudden realization hit him. His shift wouldn't be over until 6:30, and D.C. was over an hour away.

"I'll need to leave work early. Ned won't be happy," he mulled to himself, glancing at his clock, which now read 9:38 a.m.

"I'll just say I have a doctor's appointment," he muttered as he got to his feet, went to his room, grabbed his work attire and swiftly got dressed.

"Becky," he called out as he left his room and approached the virtual mate device, softly humming on the shelf.

"Hey Connor," she replied, materializing in front of him, causing him to startle slightly. He wondered if he could ever get used to her sudden appearances.

"Off to work?" she inquired.

"Yeah," he confirmed with a nod. "I'm also meeting another friend afterward, so I'm not sure when I'll be back," he added.

For a moment, Becky's digital avatar seemed to darken slightly before she cheerfully responded.

"I heard. You're going to Washington D.C.! The capital of the United States! That sounds fun!" she replied cheerfully. "I wish I could go with you," she added.

"Maybe another time," Connor responded. "I have to go, but I'll see you later," he said as he ventured toward the door.

"OK, Connor, I'll be here when you get home," she said before vanishing from sight.

Connor breathed a sigh of relief and hurried out the door, locking it behind him. Descending the stairs, he jumped into his car, the engine letting out a prolonged squeal that grated on his nerves.

"I really have to get that fixed," he muttered to himself as he backed out of his spot. After a brief struggle with the shifter, he engaged the gear and headed to work.

* * *

He arrived at work a few minutes ahead of his scheduled start time, smoothly pulling into his usual parking spot next to Bob, the inflatable salesman. Stepping out of his car, he briskly headed toward the entrance.

Upon entering, his eyes caught the real Becky Anderson engrossed in a conversation with a customer. As he passed by, she shot him a quick, alluring glance, her hand gracefully tucking a strand of hair behind her ear. The mere sight of her had him on cloud nine, and time seemed to slow down.

Completely lost in her gaze, he made his way toward the time card machine at the back of the store, blissfully oblivious to his surroundings. His hand instinctively rose to wave at Becky, but her expression suddenly shifted from happiness to concern. Bewildered, he soon realized why when he bumped into his boss, Ned, who'd been standing in his path, arms crossed, with his right foot tapping impatiently.

Connor took a step back and redirected his attention to Ned, offering an apologetic, "Oh, sorry Ned. Didn't see you there," as he tried to maneuver around his boss. However, Ned moved to block his path.

"You know what my father used to say to me when I was your age?" Ned quipped, spittle flying from his lips with each word.

Connor flinched slightly before responding, "Uh, no?"

Ned continued, "He used to say, 'Son, if you're early, you're on time. If you're on time, you're late!'"

Connor blinked, trying to make sense of Ned's words. Hoping to diffuse the tension, he said, "Uh... okay?"

"It means," Ned clarified, "if you're not early, you're late."

Connor nodded slowly, eyes flicking around as he processed it. "Right... I think I get it now," he said, thinking aloud. "So, you want me to show up earlier?"

"I want you to *want* to show up earlier," Ned shot back with a smirk. "Show a little initiative. Don't you want to be a manager like me someday?" he asked as he stood squarely in Connor's path.

Connor hadn't really contemplated becoming a manager but was now giving it some thought.

"Absolutely," Connor replied, his head nodding thoughtfully as he considered the possibility. "Someday, perhaps."

Ned placed his hands on Connor's shoulders, and their eyes locked in a meaningful gaze. "I see potential in you," Ned said.

Connor battled to conceal his astonishment. "You, you do?" he inquired hesitantly.

"Yes, I do," Ned affirmed, giving Connor's shoulders a light shake before crossing his arms once more. "You just need to show a little more initiative, and who knows?" Ned advised.

Connor nodded, pondering Ned's words. "Okay, Ned, I'll try from now on," he promised. "Now I've got to go clock in, or I'll be late!" he exclaimed, glancing at the time inching closer to 10 a.m.

"Go on," Ned replied, stepping aside, allowing Connor to pass.

"Thanks," Connor said as he hurried toward the double doors, making his way to the time card machine.

Suddenly, he remembered his meeting with Trix. "Oh, by the way, I have to leave a little early today," Connor added, turning back toward Ned, who was now looking at him as if peering into his soul.

"For what reason?" Ned inquired, his eyes narrowing suspiciously, his arms crossed once more.

"I have a doctor's appointment," Connor replied, scratching his head. "It was last minute," he added nervously, hoping Ned wouldn't see through his ruse.

"What time do you have to leave?" Ned inquired after a moment.

Connor quickly considered how long it would take to get to Washington D.C., and realized it was a little over an hour drive.

"I need to leave by 4:30," he responded, his heart starting to race in his chest as Ned tilted his head thoughtfully while he considered Connor's words for what seemed like an eternity.

"Very well," Ned replied, his tone firm. "Just make sure you bring a doctor's note on your next shift."

"You got it, Ned," Connor responded before turning back and pushing through the double doors, moving swiftly toward the time card machine. There, he retrieved his card and punched in at 9:59 a.m., breathing a sigh of relief as he returned the card to its designated slot.

He wondered where he was going to get a doctor's note to show Ned, but decided he'd cross that bridge when he got to it.

"Yo, Con–man! What's up buddy!" came the familiar voice of Jake, catching Connor off guard, and making him flinch slightly.

"Hey, Jake," he replied, turning to face his friend.

Jake stared at Connor as if seeing him with fresh eyes. "So," Jake began. "How'd it go with Becky?" he asked quietly, scanning the surroundings for potential eavesdroppers and nudging Connor with his elbow.

Connor hesitated for a moment before responding, "It, uh… It went well, I guess," as he skillfully maneuvered around Jake and headed toward the men's room.

"No way, bro! Spill the details!" Jake called out after him.

Connor didn't turn but shouted from the restroom entrance, "No details!" before entering the restroom and closing the door behind him.

Jake simply laughed and said, "Aw, man! Alright!" before returning to his work, stacking pallets nearby.

Meanwhile, in the restroom, Connor strolled over to the sink, turning on the hot water and patiently waiting for it to reach the desired temperature. As the water flowed, he caught his reflection in the mirror. Memories of his experiences with both the real and digital incarnations of Becky Anderson flickered through his mind.

His thoughts then drifted to the news article about the Japanese man murdered by his own virtual partner. Cupping warm water in his hands, he splashed it on his face, studying his reflection as droplets trickled down his cheeks. Mentally urging himself to endure the upcoming shift and rendezvous with Trix, he reached for a paper towel to dry his face.

Tossing it in the trash, he exited the men's room to find Becky waiting.

"Hey there," she greeted him cheerfully. "Everything okay?" she inquired, a hint of concern crossing her face.

"Yeah, everything's fine," Connor assured her. "Why?" he asked, noticing

Jake momentarily pausing his tasks to smile and give him a thumbs-up.

"Well, I overheard you mentioning a doctor's appointment," she explained. "So, I got a bit worried."

"Ah, that, uh…" he started as he noticed Jake now being goofy behind Becky. "That's just a routine checkup," Connor responded, suppressing a grin as he saw Jake engaging in comical gestures while thrusting his hips in a mock display in the background.

"Okay, but you said it was a last-minute appointment," Becky pointed out, genuine concern reflected in her eyes.

Despite Jake's distracting antics, Connor focused on framing his response. "Yes, the uh doctor, stressed the importance of a prompt visit," he reassured her, his attention once again drawn to Jake's theatrical display.

This time, Jake turned his back toward them, wrapping his arms around himself as if engaged in a casual make-out session with some unseen person.

Connor tried not to laugh as he responded, "My doctor felt it'd been too long since my last checkup."

Becky's initial concern eased as she responded, "Oh. so, they just wanted to see you ASAP?"

"Yeah, exactly," Connor added, holding out his arms while keeping a straight face, despite Jake's ongoing performance.

Becky, noticing Connor's attention wavering, turned toward Jake, who suddenly adopted an innocent look, pretending to gaze at the rafters, while pointing at some unseen problem and mumbling to himself.

Resisting a chuckle, Connor regained his composure as Becky refocused on him. Leaning in closer, she whispered, "So, it's not about last night?"

Realizing the source of her concern, Connor quickly reassured her, "Oh no no no no no, nothing like that. It's just a uh… a routine cholesterol check," he calmly explained, glancing again at Jake's resumed antics.

"Okay, good," she responded with a relieved sigh.

"Yeah, no worries," he reassured her. "Last night was perfect," he added quietly, gazing into her eyes while making an effort to disregard Jake's tomfoolery.

"It really was, wasn't it?" she inquired, moving closer and gently touching his hand. "Can I see you again soon?" she whispered, their fingers intertwining.

Connor felt his heart flutter as he looked into her green eyes. "Yeah, definitely," he responded, now completely absorbed in the moment, his thoughts of Jake momentarily fading away.

"Tonight?" she asked, releasing his hand and stepping back slightly.

"Can't tonight," he replied, recalling his prior commitment to a meet-up with Trix a few hours from now.

"How about tomorrow? I'm off," he suggested, his attention wavering once again to Jake's ongoing theatrics.

"It's a date," she concurred, pulling a purple permanent marker from her pocket and gently taking hold of his hand. "Here's my number," she added, inscribing it on the skin of his wrist. "Give me a call later?" she requested, deftly stashing the marker back in her pocket.

"Sure thing," he replied, unfazed by Jake's ongoing antics.

"Cut it out, Jake," Becky exclaimed, quickly turning and redirecting her attention toward Jake.

"What?" he asked innocently as she briskly moved past him, pushing through the double doors that led to the sales floor.

Connor glanced at the message scrawled on his inner arm: *Call me! 555-1432*, with two small heart shapes drawn on either side.

"Hot damn, Con-man!" Jake exclaimed, suddenly appearing beside Connor. "You and Becks becoming a thing or what?" he inquired.

Connor pondered Jake's words as he stared at the doors Becky had just passed through. "I don't know," he replied. "Maybe," he added.

"Well, congrats, buddy!" Jake responded, giving Connor a friendly pat on the shoulder. "She's a keeper," he added.

"Thanks, Jake," Connor said, thinking about his upcoming meeting with his best online friend, Trix. "Well, time to make the donuts!" he declared, pushing through the double doors to the sales floor.

"Go get 'em, tiger," Jake muttered to himself, turning back to his duty of sorting stock and stacking pallets.

* * *

Connor completed the remainder of his shift, diligently restocking movies, magazines, and other items while occasionally exchanging smiles with Becky. As the clock ticked away, eventually, 4:30 arrived, signaling the early end of his workday.

Finding Ned in his office, a space that more closely resembled a broom closet, engrossed in spreadsheets, Connor announced his departure from the doorway. "Hey, I'm heading out now," he informed Ned, who paused, glanced at the clock on the wall, and responded, "Alright, don't forget my doctor's note," before returning to his paperwork.

Connor felt a sense of relief as he briskly made his way to the time card machine. Punching out at precisely 4:31, he slid his card back into its designated slot. Striding through the double doors, he headed toward the exit, where he spotted Becky doing her rounds.

"Leaving now?" she inquired.

"Yeah, gotta go. But I'll call you later! I Promise!" he assured her.

"Okay, you better," she replied with a smile and a wink, resuming her duties with other customers.

"Oh, I will, don't you worry," he whispered under his breath as he exited Tech & More.

Climbing into his vehicle, he ignited the engine. The radio filled the air with the familiar notes of *Sweet Home Alabama* as he declared, "D.C., here I come!"

He wrestled briefly with the gearshift before it finally clicked into place, the loose drive belt answering with its familiar high-pitched squeal. "Really gotta get that fixed," he muttered, guiding the car out of the Tech & More parking lot.

Merging onto the main road, he settled into the rhythm of traffic, the city lights stretching behind as he headed toward the highway—and toward his friend.

* * *

Meanwhile, back at Tech & More, Jake approached Becky, curious about Connor's early departure.

"Uh, hey Becks," he greeted her as she meticulously cleaned a glass case displaying various video camera models.

"Hey Jake," she replied with a subtle sigh, continuing her cleaning. "What's up?" she added.

"Just wondering what's up with Connor," he inquired, catching her attention.

"What about him?" she asked, a suspicious look on her face.

"Oh, I was just wondering if he was alright. He left early," he explained.

"He's fine, as far as I know. Just had a doctor's appointment," she said, resuming her cleaning.

"Hmm," Jake pondered. "So, are you two a thing now, or what?" he asked, shifting the subject and causing her to pause again.

"That's really none of your business, Jake," she retorted, turning toward him with a mildly annoyed expression.

"Whoa, OK, sorry I asked," he apologized as she continued cleaning. "I just remember you telling me once upon a time that you don't date coworkers," he added after a moment, making her pause once more, her eyes scanning the glass case in front of her.

She took a deep breath and turned toward him.

"Look, Jake," she said, meeting his eyes. "I think you're a great guy."

"But?" Jake asked.

She hesitated, then looked back to the glass case, resuming her cleaning. "But you're just not my type."

Jake's jaw hung open. "And Connor is?" he asked incredulously, his arms now crossed.

Becky stopped cleaning again. She stared at the glass, lost in thought. "I don't know," she responded after a moment. "Maybe," she added, continuing to clean.

Jake studied her for a moment, then nodded approvingly. "Okay then, but if you break his heart, you'll answer to me," he said half-jokingly, jabbing his thumb toward his chest, and eliciting an incredulous laugh from Becky.

"Okay?" she replied as he made his way through the swinging double doors.

Becky stared at the closing doors, her thoughts drifting to Connor. "Maybe," she whispered under her breath with a smile, resuming her task of spraying and wiping down the glass camera case.

* * *

Some time later, Connor exited the highway. He stopped at a red light and grabbed the printed instructions from his passenger seat.

"Okay, where are we going?" he asked himself as he read the directions instructing him to continue straight for a few blocks before turning right, where his destination awaited a half–mile down the road.

"Not far now," he muttered as the light turned green and he drove on. Within minutes he'd arrived at the Twisted Tail Tavern, a dive if he ever saw one.

The sign on the awning depicted an image of the Cheshire Cat from the *Alice in Wonderland* stories, with a black and white striped tail twisted in a knot, and a tankard of ale splashing around in its hand as it smiled deviously.

"This must be the place," he mused as he searched for a spot to park.

It was street parking only, and so far, no spots were empty. It was a busy night at the Twisted Tail.

"C'mon, there's gotta be somewhere to park," he lamented as he drove slowly, looking for a spot, when suddenly, he spotted a car leaving.

As it left, he pulled ahead and backed in, turning the rear of his car in order to squeeze into the space, missing the car in front of him by mere inches.

"Like a glove," he mused as he turned off his car and hopped out, closing his door. He could hear music coming from within.

As he reached for the door, another patron pushed it open from inside, nearly hitting Connor.

"Oh, excshuuse me," the patron slurred as he swayed to and fro, emitting the occasional hiccup.

"So sorry about that," he continued drunkenly.

"It's OK, no problem man," Connor replied.

This seemed to satisfy the drunken patron, who offered a friendly nod.

"I'll just be on my way then," he slurred again as he turned and stumbled his way down the sidewalk to some unknown destination.

Connor watched to see if he was about to get into a car, but to his relief, the guy just kept walking.

"Geez," Connor muttered under his breath as he turned and entered the Twisted Tail.

Entering the establishment, he took in the scene. *Bad to the Bone* by George Thorogood was playing from the jukebox through a built-in sound system with speakers installed strategically throughout the tavern. There were a few tables and booths where patrons sat drinking and smoking. There was also a wraparound bar where more customers sat watching a football game on the TV screen. The Philadelphia Eagles were playing against the Dallas Cowboys.

The bartender, a woman in her fifties, sporting a dark shirt with a jean jacket vest covered in all manner of patches that looked to Connor like various biker logos or insignias, watched him enter.

Connor looked at the patrons sitting at the bar one by one and realized he had no idea what Trix even looked like. He decided to ask the bartender.

"What can I get ya?" she inquired, finishing with a glass and setting it back in its designated spot.

"I'm uh, looking for a friend," he responded.

"Okay," she replied. "Your friend got a name?" she asked, setting her hands on the bar.

He briefly wondered why he'd forgotten to ask Trix what his real name might be.

"Uhm," he hesitated. "He goes by Trix?" he clarified with a hint of uncertainty.

The bartender looked at him as if sizing him up before responding. "You know this guy, Trix?" she shouted, turning toward a patron sitting a few seats to Connor's left.

The man, in his mid-thirties with shoulder-length dark hair, reading glasses, a full beard with a mustache, wearing jeans, work boots, and a black button–down long–sleeved shirt, turned toward her and looked at Connor while taking a sip of his beer.

"Yep, he's with me," Trix replied as he waved Connor over.

Connor felt relieved to finally put a face to the name.

"Hey man," Connor greeted as he approached.

"Hey broham! Welcome to the capital!" Trix added, putting his hand out for a shake.

Connor grasped Trix's hand, and Trix gave it a good shake and squeeze, which felt to Connor as if he was trying to crush his hand.

"Have a seat," Trix said, gesturing to the stool beside him. As soon as Connor sat down, Trix caught the bartender's attention.

"Hey, Margie!" he called. "Uno cerveza for mi amigo here, eh?"

Margie gave an amused nod, grabbed a glass, and filled it from the tap. She slid it across the counter, setting it neatly on a coaster in front of Connor.

"Thanks, man," Connor said.

"Don't thank me—you're paying for it," Trix replied with a grin.

"Right," Connor chuckled, remembering their earlier conversation.

"Cheers, broham," Trix said, raising his glass. Connor lifted his own, and their beers met with a soft *clink* before both took a long, satisfying drink.

"Ahhh," Trix sighed after gulping down his beer.

"So, what's going on, man?" Trix inquired with a curious look.

Connor laid out the situation while Trix listened and drank.

* * *

By the time Connor finished his tale, they were midway through their fourth round of beers.

Trix simply stared at him in disbelief. "You know how crazy this all sounds, right?" he asked after a pause.

"Yeah, I do," Connor replied, sipping his beer. "I think I'm in trouble, man."

"Yeah, it sounds like you might be," Trix replied.

They each took a slow sip of beer, the silence between them thick with unspoken thoughts.

After a moment, Trix glanced over and asked, "Have you tried just shutting it off?"

"I thought about it, but what if she figures out what I'm doing and tries to stop me? Violently?" Connor replied.

"Yeah, that could be a problem," Trix admitted.

"Plus, I'm not even sure I can shut it down. It's self–powered, and the instructions don't mention how to turn it off," Connor added.

"Got any ideas?" he asked.

"Well, generally speaking, an electromagnetic pulse will disable anything electronic, so there's that," Trix said. "The problem is figuring out how to make one."

"Do you know how?" Connor asked.

Trix shrugged. "Well, you could set off a nuclear blast in the upper atmosphere—but ideally, you want something tiny and targeted that does the job without frying the whole neighborhood or causing a mass panic." They both chuckled at the absurdity of it.

After a moment, Trix looked as if he'd suddenly had an epiphany. "Hmm, I wonder," he muttered, grabbing a napkin and a pen from his pocket. He began to draw.

Connor leaned in for a closer look. It appeared to be a rough sketch of a device—cylindrical capacitors arranged in a pattern, lines connecting them to mark electrical pathways, with tiny "+" and "–" symbols scattered throughout.

He watched as Trix added a few more shapes, his pen moving swiftly across the napkin.

"There," Trix said finally, sitting back with a grin. "This oughta do it." He slid the napkin across the counter toward Connor.

"What is it?" Connor asked, turning it around in an attempt to make sense of the drawing.

"It should do the trick," Trix replied before leaning in closer, lowering his voice. "It'll generate a small electromagnetic pulse that should disable your problem. Just keep in mind that setting off an EMP is highly illegal and could land you in federal prison, so that being said, you didn't get this idea from me."

Connor's thoughts briefly flashed to an image of himself being perp-walked into a federal prison, inmates behind the fence hooting and hollering, shouting things like 'fresh fish' and catcalling him. Connor nodded in understanding.

"I understand," he said with a gulp as he studied the rough sketch.

Trix grabbed another napkin and began writing a list numbered 1, 2, etc.

"And, here's a list of the parts you'll need," he clarified as he wrote down the ingredients for the device. "You should be able to get all of this stuff at Electronics Shack," he said, handing the list to Connor who took it and nodded.

"Just round up those parts and put it together according to the drawing and you should be good to go," Trix stated before taking another sip of his beer.

"I don't know how to thank you," Connor said as he took another drink.

"What're bros for?" Trix replied, raising his hand to get the bartender's attention.

"Hey Margie, another round please!" Trix shouted, holding up two fingers.

"You got it, Trix," she replied as she worked on their drinks.

Connor glanced at a clock on the wall; it read 9:42. Realizing he'd lost track of time, he decided to call it a night.

"Last one for me, then I gotta go," Connor said, placing his credit card on the bar to cover their tab.

"Are you going home?" Trix inquired. "Is that safe?" he added.

"Where else am I gonna go?" Connor replied, taking another swig of his beer.

"You can crash at my place, broham," Trix offered. "I live right up the street," he added. "Besides, I wouldn't want you driving in your condition. I need my warfield buddy," he said, raising his beer glass before taking another swig.

Connor stood up and felt a little light-headed, realizing he might have had too much to drink.

"Okay, man," he slurred slightly before sitting back down. "I appreciate it," he added as Trix signaled the bartender for the check.

"No problemo, mi amigo," Trix responded as Margie brought them another round of beer, which they clinked and drank.

Afterwards, Trix supported Connor as they exited the bar and walked down the street toward Trix's home. Connor was drunkenly slurring his words, leaning on Trix for stability.

"I think I'm in love with this girl," he said, prompting Trix to offer the same response as the last time Connor had mentioned it, minutes prior.

"I know, broham, I know," he said as they rounded the corner and arrived at Trix's residence—a unit in a row home where multiple units formed one long structure.

"Home sweet home," Trix said as they reached the gated entrance to his modest front yard.

"Hang on a second," Trix added, punching in his gate code to unlock the mechanism. They both made their way up the small walkway to his front door.

As Trix jingled his keys in the lock, Connor glanced around and noticed the small pond in Trix's front yard.

"You have a pond in your front yard?" he remarked as Trix opened the door.

"Yep," Trix replied as he led them both inside and closed the door.

"Alright, broham," Trix said as he led Connor to his couch and helped him lay down. "You can sleep here. I'll get you a blanket and pillow," he added, turning to head upstairs to fetch the bedding.

Connor settled on the sofa and closed his eyes.

Trix returned a few moments later with a blanket and pillow.

"Here you go," he said, handing the bedding to Connor.

"Thanks, man," Connor responded, laying down and turning onto his side.

"No problem, dude," Trix offered, noticing Connor was already snoring.

"Sleep tight, broham," Trix added as he turned and headed upstairs to his room, shutting off the lights as he went.

Soon, Connor drifted into slumber and found himself immersed in another dream. In this nocturnal realm, he stood within the confines of his condo, positioned near the foot of the staircase that ascended to his second–floor abode. The moon cast an ethereal glow, painting the surroundings in shadows while the nearby crickets orchestrated a symphony of chirps.

Perplexed, he muttered, "How did I get here?"

Just then, the sound of approaching footsteps caught his attention. He turned to see Becky, clad in denim jeans, a jean jacket, and Converse sneakers.

"Becky?" he uttered in surprise as she halted and extracted a piece of paper from her pocket. Without a word, she scrutinized the information inscribed upon it, featuring Connor's address scrawled in ink. Lifting her gaze, she espied a sign labeled "2A—2J" with an arrow directing upward toward his dwelling.

Passing by Connor without acknowledgment, she ascended the flight of steps toward his door.

"Wait, Becky!" he called out, his pleas falling on deaf ears as she made no indication of hearing him.

As she reached his threshold, she confirmed the apartment number before rapping lightly on the door. An apprehensive sigh escaped Connor as he observed the unfolding scene.

Becky attempted the doorknob, which yielded with a protracted creak.

"Connor?" she called out into the darkness of the apartment. "Are you there?" she queried once more, but was met with silence. Resolute, she ventured further into Connor's domain, repeating her inquiry.

Suddenly, the digital replication of Becky manifested behind her corporeal form.

"Connor is currently out," the electronic doppelganger informed, causing Becky to startle as she turned toward the unexpected voice.

"However, perhaps I can provide some assistance," Becky's digital avatar continued as she extended a hand to shut the door.

Connor's last glimpse was of Becky's startled visage as the door sealed shut.

"Becky!" Connor called out as he stirred awake on his friend's couch. Glancing around, he realized it'd all been a dream.

"Aaahhh," he groaned, feeling the pounding sensation of a headache settling in. "Too much to drink," he lamented, sitting up on the unfamiliar couch.

The morning sun had risen, casting light into Trix's tidy abode. Glancing at a clock on the wall, he noted it was 8:42 a.m. Rubbing his temples to clear his head, he observed, "Certainly nicer than my place," before making his way to the kitchen.

Trix remained asleep, so Connor quietly rummaged through the cabinets in search of a glass. He filled it from Trix's refrigerator water dispenser and took a long, refreshing gulp.

"Ahhh," he sighed with relief, refilling his glass and drinking again. "So thirsty," he muttered, promising himself, "I'm never drinking again," as he returned to the couch.

"How're you feeling, broham?" asked Trix, now awake and clad in a robe, as he descended the stairs.

"I'll live, I think," Connor replied as he rubbed his throbbing temples.

"Here, thought you could use this," Trix added, handing Connor a small blue pill.

"Thanks," Connor replied, accepting the offering. "What's this?" he asked, scrutinizing the pill.

"It's an anti–inflammatory," Trix explained. "Good for headaches."

"Coffee?" Trix offered, already heading to the coffee machine.

"Yeah, I could go for some coffee," Connor agreed, settling onto a stool at Trix's breakfast bar.

"Sugar and cream?" Trix asked as he grabbed two mugs from the cabinet and poured coffee for them both.

"Yes, please," Connor replied, pinching the bridge of his nose in a futile attempt to dull the pounding in his head.

He briefly pictured a small gnome inside his skull, solemnly smacking the inside of his head with a tiny war hammer, as if it were his sworn duty.

Trix added sugar and cream before bringing Connor his coffee and setting it in front of him. "So, how'd you sleep?" he asked, taking a sip of his own.

"Not too bad," Connor replied, popping the blue pill and washing it down with his coffee. He winced as it burned his tongue. "Just been having bad dreams lately."

"Anything in particular?" Trix probed, sipping his coffee.

"Mostly about this virtual mate thing," Connor confessed, wincing again as he sipped the hot coffee.

"This is why I never beta test anything," Trix remarked, earning a chuckle from both of them.

"Yeah, tell me about it," Connor agreed, blowing on his coffee to cool it down. "Never again, I'll tell you that much," he added after another sip.

"Never say never, broham" Trix countered, finishing his coffee and rinsing his cup in the sink.

"So, I've thought about it," Trix said, placing his hands on the counter. "And it occurs to me that you might actually need my help to build this thing."

"Yeah, probably," Connor agreed with a nod, while taking another tentative sip of his coffee.

"So, I'm gonna help you build it," Trix continued.

"Really?" Connor asked, surprised.

"Of course," Trix replied, holding out his fist. "What're bros for, broham?"

"Thanks, man," Connor said, bumping his fist against Trix's.

"You're a real life saver," Connor said, finishing his coffee.

"Don't I know it," Trix remarked as he took Connors mug, rinsed it in the sink and placed it in the drying rack.

"Alright, I'm gonna go toss some clothes on and be right back," he announced, heading upstairs to dress.

Minutes later, they were both ready to go.

"Let's go, you're driving," Trix declared as they exited the house, making their way a few blocks to Connor's car, which was still parked near the Twisted Tail.

As they reached it, they quickly hopped in and fired up the engine, which emitted a long squeal.

"Nice ride," Trix said, as Connor wrestled with the shifter to get it into gear.

"Thanks," Connor replied, finally managing to shift into first gear. "And we're off," he said as they drove off.

* * *

After navigating winding roads and various intersections, they finally arrived at Electronics Shack. The small shop appeared to have been established for quite some time, with an alley leading to a rear parking lot where Connor smoothly maneuvered his car. Cutting the engine, they stepped out and entered the store through the rear entrance. As they crossed the threshold, an electronic door chime emitted a gentle *ding–dong*.

Scanning the store, they searched for the section likely to house the components they needed, but it quickly became apparent that most of the stock was kept behind the counter on various shelves arranged in aisles.

As they made their way toward the counter, an elderly man in black khakis and a red button–down shirt, adorned with a name tag that read *Peter,* emerged from one of the aisles, offering them a warm smile.

"Welcome to Electronics Shack, how can I assist you, gentlemen?" he greeted kindly.

"Got the list?" Trix asked Connor.

"Oh, oh, yeah, right," Connor responded, retrieving the napkin from his pocket where Trix had jotted down the ingredients for the device. "Right here," he said, passing the napkin to the elderly man, who reminded Connor of Santa Claus with his shaggy white hair and thick white beard.

Donning his glasses, the man scrutinized the list while Connor and Trix watched attentively. "Interesting list," the shopkeeper remarked, peering up at them above the lenses of his glasses, which sat perched on his nose. "What're you boys making?" he inquired, reaching for his sales slip pad and a pen.

"Well," Connor began, but Trix interjected smoothly, "It's for a science fair project."

"Yeah, it's a science fair project," Connor agreed, nodding.

"Aren't you two a bit old for that sort of thing?" the elderly man asked, persisting.

"It's for his girlfriend's kid," Trix offered calmly, attempting to halt the questioning.

"Okay, just wondering," the old man insisted. "I'll gather these up for you and be back in a jiffy," he added, retreating to one of the aisles where the stock was kept.

"My girlfriend's kid?" Connor whispered to Trix once the shopkeeper had left.

"Yeah, don't worry about it," Trix replied discreetly. "Just don't mention anything about EMP's, okay? Remember, this sort of thing is not exactly legal," he added quietly, leaning closer so only Connor could hear.

Connor nodded in understanding, though his mind once again wandered to an unsettling vision: a cramped jail cell door slamming shut while other inmates shouted *Fresh Fish!* over and over.

"Well, here you are," the elderly man returned, interrupting Connor's unpleasant thoughts, their order now fulfilled. He'd packed all the components into a brown paper bag and was now ringing them up.

"Okay gentlemen, that'll be $27.42," he stated as the cash register drawer opened with a *cha-ching*.

"Oh, right," Connor realized, retrieving his wallet. He pulled it open, grabbed his debit card, and handed it to the shopkeeper, who deftly swiped it in his credit card machine before handing it back.

After a moment, the payment authorization came through, and a slip printed, requiring Connor's signature.

"Just need you to sign here," the elderly man quipped, placing the slip on the counter with a pen, reaching for the second copy that was now printing.

Connor quickly scribbled his signature on the designated line and handed it back. The man stapled the second copy to the brown paper bag before handing it over.

"Have a nice day," he smiled.

"Thanks, you too," Connor replied as they left the store, setting off the *ding-dong* chime once more.

As they reached his waiting car, they opened the doors and hopped in.

"We'll put it together back at my place," Trix said, snapping his seat belt into place.

"Thanks, man. I really appreciate this," Connor replied, starting the engine. The belts squealed in protest.

"No problemo, Broham!" Trix grinned. "This should be fun!"

Connor felt a surge of gratitude for having Trix as a friend. Backing out of the parking spot, he shifted into gear with minimal struggle and headed back toward Trix's abode.

* * *

Shortly after, they arrived at Trix's home.

"Park over there," Trix directed, pointing to an empty spot adjacent to his unit.

Connor skillfully maneuvered his car into the designated space and turned off the engine. Carrying their load, they entered the house.

"Let's use the table," Trix suggested, nodding toward his dining area.

The table was a circular one crafted from faux wood with steel legs, surrounded by several chairs.

"I'll be back in a minute," Trix announced as Connor settled into a chair.

"Alright," Connor replied, unpacking the components onto the table.

As he spread them out, he realized he had no clue about their functions or how they would integrate.

"Geez, I don't think I'd ever be able to put this together," he mumbled to himself.

Trix returned shortly with a small plastic case and an articulated magnifying glass, complete with its own stand. Placing them on the table, he took a seat beside Connor.

Opening the case revealed a home soldering kit.

Setting up his kit, Trix plugged in the soldering iron and placed it in the holder to warm it up.

"Okay, Just gotta let that warm up for a few minutes," Trix remarked, retrieving the napkin diagram from the table to study it.

After a moment, Trix put down the napkin and reached for the nearest component—a piece resembling a circuit board with dangling wires—and began his work.

Connor watched in amazement as Trix deftly wielded the soldering iron to swiftly connect the various components, occasionally asking Connor to hand him parts.

"Hand me those thermistors," Trix remarked, soldering a component onto the main board.

Connor glanced at the assortment of components on the table, feeling puzzled.

"It's that plastic baggie with the little black balloon–shaped things," Trix clarified, pointing to the bag.

"Ah," Connor replied, finally understanding, and handed the bag to Trix.

Trix retrieved two of the balloon–shaped components and positioned them in their designated spots before soldering them into place. Smoke emanated each time, carrying a distinct pine scent that Connor tried to avoid inhaling.

After what felt like hours to Connor, Trix finally completed the device.

"All set," Trix declared with a hint of triumph in his voice, as he placed the completed device on the table.

"It's done?" Connor inquired.

"Yep," Trix confirmed, unplugging his soldering tool and packing away his kit.

Connor eyed the device but refrained from touching it, worried he might accidentally damage it. It resembled the old metal detectors he recalled using as a child, though much smaller, just over a foot in length, featuring a single handle grip and a metal box attached about six inches up. The box housed a red light, a toggle switch, and a red button roughly the size of a quarter. Above that, an antenna was affixed.

"Crazy," Connor muttered. "Will it work?" he asked after a moment.

"Only one way to find out, but here's the thing," Trix began.

"This thing is one time use. Meaning, once you use it, that's it. Comprende?"

"Understood," Connor replied.

"Okay, so now that that's out of the way, here's how you use it," Trix continued. "First, you flip this switch up," he said, pointing to the silver toggle switch. "Then, just make sure you're within a few feet of this virtual mate device and hit the big red button."

"And that's it?" Connor queried.

"That's it," Trix confirmed. "It'll disable any electronic device within a few feet, but only once. Understood?"

"Understood," Connor replied with a slight gulp. He picked up the device, marveling at its design.

"Thanks again, man," he said, placing it back on the table.

"No problemo, mi amigo," Trix reassured him. "Like I always say—what're bros for, broham?"

"Yeah," Connor acknowledged, checking the time. "4:46 p.m. I'd better head home soon," he said, suddenly remembering his promise to call Becky.

"Shit!" he exclaimed.

"What's wrong?" Trix asked.

Connor sighed, "I promised Becky I'd call her last night and I completely forgot!"

"Yeah, sounds like you need to sort that out," Trix remarked. "You want to give her a call? You can use my phone," he offered.

"Are you sure?" Connor hesitated.

"Of course, broham! I'll not stand in the way of true love." Trix gestured at the phone near the refrigerator.

"Thanks, dude," Connor replied, dialing Becky's number.

After a few rings, someone answered, "Hello, Anderson residence."

"Uh hi! Is uh, Becky there?" Connor asked awkwardly.

"No, she's not home at the moment, can I take a message?"

"Could you let her know that Connor called," he said.

"Connor? Okay, I'll let her know," came the response.

"Thanks and have a great evening," Connor replied.

"You too," said the voice before the line clicked.

"Wasn't home, eh?" Trix remarked as Connor replaced the phone.

"No," Connor replied with a sigh. "I'd better head back."

"Okay, bro, it's been fun," Trix said as they rose to their feet. "Let's do this again sometime."

"Yeah, definitely," Connor agreed. "If I survive," he added with a nervous chuckle.

"You're gonna be fine," Trix reassured him. "Just remember what I told you."

"Got it," Connor said, grabbing the homemade EMP device and heading for the door.

"Don't die," Trix joked as Connor stepped outside.

Connor turned to see Trix leaning in the doorway, arms crossed. "I need my warfield buddy," Trix reminded him, miming gunshots with his finger.

"Thanks, I'll try not to," Connor replied with a grin, then headed toward his car.

He hopped in, turned the key, and the engine started with a long squeal. As he maneuvered out of the spot and headed home, Trix watched him go.

"Don't die, dude," he muttered before heading back inside.

As he walked through the kitchen, something caught his eye on the chair Connor had been sitting in.

"Hmm? What's this?" he wondered, picking up a wallet. "A wallet?" he said, opening it and finding Connor's driver's license inside.

"Oh shit," he exclaimed, rushing to the front door, but Connor was already gone.

"Figures," Trix sighed, heading back inside and closing the door behind him.

* * *

Meanwhile, back at the Urban Oasis, Ebenezer Abramowitz—Connor's cigar-smoking landlord— relaxed on his first-floor patio, a modest 8×6-foot screened-in space. The patio was sparsely furnished with an old recliner, a small end table with a lamp, and a large faux crystal ashtray overflowing with a week's worth of cigar butts. It overlooked the parking lot, giving him a clear view of everyone coming and going. As he sat reclined in his chair, flipping through *The Dover Dirt Gazette*—a local tabloid known for its gossip and sensationalism—he occasionally let out a deep, gravelly cough—a reminder of his less-than-stellar health.

The sun had already set, and the streetlights flickered on, casting long shadows over the complex and signaling the neighborhood kids to head home for the night.

It was Saturday, and Ebenezer was keeping an eye out for Connor, who'd promised to pay the rent by the weeks end. Connor was usually home on

Saturdays, so Ebenezer expected to see him soon.

As he flipped through the tabloid, a headline caught his eye: *Aspen Man, 24, Killed by Rogue AI*. The article described a gruesome crime scene where a 24–year–old Colorado man had been found brutally dismembered by an advanced holographic AI device that was now being recalled by a Japanese company known as VM-Corp. Ebenezer scoffed, shaking his head. "Where do they come up with this crap?" he muttered, turning the page to a story titled: *Top Secret UFO Files: The Secrets the Government Doesn't Want You to Know!* "Hmm," he uttered.

Just then, he noticed a car pulling into a spot usually reserved for visitors. Looking up, he saw that it was a convertible, cherry–red Volkswagen Beetle with white–walled tires and round silver hubcaps. Ebenezer was good at remembering details about cars and people in his vicinity, but he didn't recognize this one. As the driver parked, the engine and headlights clicked off. From his dimly lit patio, he watched to see who would emerge, certain no one could see him in return.

A young woman stepped out and closed the door. She had long blonde hair with curled ends and was wearing jeans, a windbreaker jacket, and sneakers. "Pretty girl," he remarked to himself. She reached into her pocket, pulled out a piece of paper, glanced at it, then looked up at the apartment complex before heading toward the inner courtyard.

Curiosity got the better of Ebenezer. He set down his cigar and slipped inside, closing the sliding glass door behind him. Moving to his front window—which gave him a clear view of the central courtyard—he watched as the girl climbed the stairs to the second floor, heading straight toward Connor's apartment. Reaching his abode, she stopped, tucked the slip of paper into her pocket and knocked on the door.

"He's not home, girlie," Ebenezer muttered. If Connor had been home, Ebenezer would've noticed.

But after a moment, the door opened. The girl stood there for a few seconds, then stepped inside. Ebenezer couldn't see into Connor's apartment from his vantage point, but he kept watching anyway as she crossed the threshold and the door shut behind her.

"Huh? He's home?" Ebenezer muttered, scratching his head. He didn't recall seeing Connor come home, and since he spent most of his time smoking in his enclosed patio, he usually noticed anyone coming or going. He went out to his back porch, overlooking the parking lot, and scanned the area for Connor's vehicle. It wasn't in its usual spot, or anywhere else. "That's strange," he thought.

He started to wonder if Connor had a roommate he didn't know about. "Or maybe he's got family over," he speculated, trying to make sense of it. At the very least, he would need to find out who was staying at Connor's place. The lease clearly stated that only tenants listed on the agreement were permitted to live there, and as far as Ebenezer knew, Connor Foreman was the only one named. With a grunt, he decided to go knock on Connor's door and get some answers.

Leaving his first–floor apartment, he climbed the stairs to the second floor, making his way quietly to Connor's door. As he drew closer, sidling past Connor's front window, he attempted to catch a glimpse inside and strained to detect any sounds emanating from within. However, the drawn curtains obscured his view, leaving him only with the distant echo of dogs barking.

He reached Connor's front door and listened again. Still nothing. He knocked loud enough for anyone inside to hear, then waited.

After a few moments, the door opened, but no one was there.

Puzzled, he peered through the crack of the door to see if someone was hiding behind it, but he didn't see anything.

"Hello?" he called out, but there was no response. It was as if the place was empty.

Who opened the door? he pondered to himself.

"Mr. Foreman?" he called out as he stepped across the threshold and into Connor's abode. The apartment looked normal, nothing was out of place.

"Mr. Foreman?" he called out again.

"I'm back here!" came Connor's voice from the bedroom, startling Ebenezer.

"Oh! Uh, Mr. Foreman! You're home?" he replied. "It's Mr. Abramowitz. You said you'd have the rent money by now."

He glanced down the hallway toward the bedroom, expecting Connor to emerge with the rent money, but after a moment, there was no reply.

"Mr. Foreman?" Ebenezer called again, louder this time.

"Yeah, I have your rent money back here!" replied the voice from the bedroom, prompting him to head down the hall to get it.

As he approached Connor's bedroom door, a sense of unease crept over him. Something felt off.

"Mr. Foreman?" he said as he stood outside the door, unsure of what awaited him on the other side.

"Yeah, come on in!" came Connor's voice from within.

Ebenezer felt his heart racing, trying to convince himself that it was just Connor Foreman. A good kid, harmless.

But when he turned the knob and pushed it open, his worst fears came true. Inside, he saw the girl from the cherry-red Volkswagen Beetle tied to a chair with a gag around her mouth. Her head was slumped to the side, suggesting she was either unconscious or worse.

Ebenezer—having survived the Nazi death camps in World War II—felt his instincts immediately kick in. He quickly scanned the room for any sign of Connor, but as far as he could tell, it was just him and the girl tied to the chair.

"Mr. Foreman?" he called out again, but got no response.

He moved to the tied-up girl and tried to wake her.

"Hey!" he shouted, shaking her gently. "Are you okay?"

He checked her pulse; it was faint, but she was alive. He then tried to untie the knots, but they were intricate, more complex than anything he'd ever encountered.

"What the hell?" he muttered as he worked at the ropes.

"Connor should be home anytime now," said a female voice from behind him.

The hairs on his neck stood up as he slowly turned to face the speaker. It was the spitting image of the girl currently tied to the chair. Blinking in disbelief, his gaze shifted back to the girl in the chair, then again at her doppelganger standing before him.

"What the—" he began to say, but before he could finish, she hit him over the head with a heavy frying pan. The last thing he felt was the rush of darkness as he collapsed to the floor.

"And we're going to have a nice talk when he does," said Becky's AI–powered digital double, her voice cool and calm, as she looked down at the unconscious Becky Anderson tied to the chair.

* * *

Connor was almost home. His nerves were on edge as he pulled into his designated parking spot. He turned off the engine and sat for a moment, the EMP device he and Trix had built was resting in his lap.

Trix's words replayed in his mind: *Remember, broham, it's one–time use only.*

He nodded to himself and repeated, "One–time use only," before getting out of his car. The door needed a good slam or two to close properly.

As he turned to head toward the stairs, a cherry–red convertible Volkswagen Beetle caught his eye in the visitor's parking spot. It looked familiar, but he couldn't place it at first. Then it hit him—he'd seen it parked outside of Tech & More while sweeping the lot, and again at Becky's house when he picked her up.

It belonged to Becky, or at least he thought so.

"Becky?" he muttered to himself. "What would she be doing here?"

He couldn't find an answer to his own question and shrugged it off.

"Maybe it belongs to someone else," he reasoned as he made his way toward the steps leading to his second–floor apartment.

As he approached his door, a feeling of unease washed over him. His heart raced as he looked around to check if anyone was watching. He tightened his grip on the EMP device and took a deep breath, feeling the weight of the moment.

Seeing no one around, Connor slid his key into the lock and turned it, only to realize that his door wasn't locked.

"What the—" he started to say when the door suddenly swung open.

Becky stood there, greeting him with a warm smile, wearing jeans, her windbreaker jacket, and black sneakers.

"Well, hello there, stranger," she said.

Connor's face registered shock. The realization that the car in the lot really did belong to Becky, and that she was now in his apartment, made him feel like a deer in headlights. He stumbled to find his words.

"Uh…" he began, but Becky's gaze shifted to the crude–looking device in his left hand.

"What's that?" she inquired, curiosity in her voice.

"Uh, this?" he replied, trying to sound nonchalant. "Oh, this is just a little project my buddy Trix and I worked on," he said, hoping that would be enough.

"Oh?" Becky asked, her curiosity piqued as she examined the device. "What's it do?"

Connor's mind raced, searching for an explanation. "It's a, uh," he stammered, then blurted out the first thing that came to mind. "It's a prop!" he said.

"A prop?" she echoed, raising an eyebrow.

"Yeah! For a game—like Dungeons & Dragons—that, my friend Trix and I play," he lied, hoping it sounded convincing.

Becky seemed satisfied with his answer, giving a small nod. "Okay, are you coming in?" she asked when he lingered at the doorway longer than he'd intended.

"Uh, yeah," he replied, stepping inside and closing the door behind him.

He glanced at the shelf near the TV where he'd left the Virtual Mate device and saw that it was missing.

"Shit!" he exclaimed, looking around in a panic.

"What's wrong?" Becky asked, noticing his concern as she took a seat on the couch.

Connor, not wanting to reveal his real concern, quickly thought of an excuse. "Oh, uh, nothing," he said, glancing around as if searching for something. "I think I lost my TV remote."

"It's right there, silly," Becky giggled, pointing to the remote on the coffee table.

"Ah! So it is," he said with a relieved smile. "Thanks," he added, nodding.

"Come sit down," Becky said, patting the spot next to her on the couch.

Connor set the device on the coffee table and sat down next to Becky, still casually searching for the Virtual Mate device while trying to keep the panic out of his voice. He suddenly found himself wondering how Becky had gotten into his apartment.

"By the way, how did you get in here?" he asked, watching her reaction.

"Oh, your landlord let me in," she replied with a casual smile.

"Mr. Abramowitz?" he questioned, puzzled.

"I think that's his name," Becky replied.

"Older man. smells like cigar smoke. Ranting about the rent?" she added.

Connor suddenly remembered he was supposed to pay the rent by the weekend.

"Oh, crap!" he muttered.

"What's wrong?" she asked.

"I promised him I'd have the rent by this weekend and I forgot to pick up my check," he admitted.

Becky seemed unfazed, placing an arm around Connor's waist. "Well good news. He said not to worry about it," she said soothingly.

"He did?" Connor replied, finding it hard to believe that Mr. Abramowitz, who was usually strict about the rent, would just let it slide. "He really said that?"

"Yep!" Becky confirmed, leaning in closer. "By the way, I had a great time the other night," she said, locking eyes with him. "And I couldn't wait to see you again."

Connor felt his pulse quicken. He recalled their evening at the drive-in theater, watching the horror film, *Halloween*.

"Yeah, me too," he said, leaning in.

But as he got closer, something felt off. He'd always loved the smell of Becky's perfume, but this time there was nothing. He pulled back, trying to determine if this was really Becky Anderson or her digital duplicate.

"What's wrong?" she asked, noticing his hesitation.

"Oh, I was just wondering what you thought of the movie," he replied, probing for clues.

Becky seemed to pause, as if considering how to answer. "It was really good," she said, nodding reassuringly.

"What was your favorite part?" he asked, sensing that he might be onto something.

Becky stared at him with her emerald-green eyes, and for a moment, the air grew tense. It felt like she was searching for the right words, and Connor's instincts told him there might be more to this than it seemed.

"I honestly don't remember much about it," she responded after a long pause. "I was too busy being focused on you," she added, a sly smile etched on her face.

Connor found her explanation for not remembering the movie to be plausible, considering he didn't really recall much of it either, in no small part thanks to the intimacy they'd shared during the film.

He was about to respond when he heard a commotion from his bedroom. "What was that?" he asked, his attention drawn to the hallway.

"I didn't hear anything," Becky responded as Connor grabbed the EMP device and rose to investigate.

"I heard something," he said, before heading down the hall with Becky in tow.

"Stay behind me," he instructed her, reaching for the door handle and opening it.

The scene that met his eyes sent shivers down his spine.

Becky Anderson—the real Becky Anderson—was tied to a chair, her mouth gagged as she struggled against her bonds. In the far corner of the room on his end table sat the Virtual Mate device, its colors swirling bright red.

The real Becky—now fully awake—looked up at him, her eyes widening as she glanced past him, trying to warn him through the gag. But, her efforts were futile, as before he could react, something heavy struck him over the head.

The last thing he saw was Becky fighting to break free as he crumpled to the floor. Darkness closed in, and the red flashing lights of the Virtual Mate device flickered in his vision.

* * *

He suddenly found himself in a booth at a diner. His mother sat across from him, her smile beaming.

"Mom?" he asked.

"Hi, honey," his mom replied from across the booth.

"Where are we?" he asked, looking around in confusion.

"You don't remember this place?" she said. "I used to bring you here all the time when you were younger."

The memory of the diner his mother often took him to began resurfacing.

"Oh, wow," he said, taking it all in. "I remember."

His mother merely shook her head, smiling.

The situation in his apartment flashed in his mind, and a terrifying thought struck him.

"Oh no," he said, his voice filled with concern. "Am I dead?"

She laughed softly, her smile just as beautiful as he remembered. "No, honey, you're not dead. Not yet, anyway," she replied, reaching for his hand.

Her touch was warm and soothing.

"But you'd better do something about that girl," she added, her tone turning serious.

"I know!" he said, rubbing his eyes.

"What were you thinking, Connor Foreman?" she asked gently.

"I don't know," he replied, shame creeping into his voice. "It's just, ever since you've been gone, I've been so alone." Tears welled in his eyes.

"Oh, honey," she said soothingly, holding his hand. "You were never alone," she assured him, her smile radiating warmth as a tear slipped down her cheek. "I'm always with you." she said, reaching out to wipe away his tears.

"That Becky girl seems nice," she said after a moment. "You could do worse."

"Yeah," he said, wiping his eyes. "She's amazing."

"You be good to her, Connor Foreman," she told him.

"I will, Mom," he replied, using his shirt to dry his tears.

"It's time to wake up now, Connor," his mother suddenly interjected, her tone shifting to serious once again.

"But I want to stay a bit longer, mom," he pleaded.

She raised her hand and slapped him.

"Wake up, Connor!" she shouted.

"Mom! Please!" he begged as she hit him again.

"Wake up, Connor!"

The final slap jolted him awake. Becky's digital doppelganger was pulling her hand back for another strike when she noticed he was conscious.

"Finally!" she declared, lowering her hand. "I want you awake for this."

Connor shook his head, trying to regain full consciousness. As his vision cleared, he saw Becky's digital avatar holding a large butcher knife—the one from his kitchen block. His heart raced. He tried to stand, but his wrists and feet were bound, just like the real Becky, who was still tied up next to him. He tried to speak, but his mouth was gagged.

Taking in the scene, he noticed Mr. Abramowitz lying unconscious on the floor and briefly wondered if he was still alive. Connor's eyes darted to the EMP device lying on the floor near the door, just out of reach.

Can't reach it, he thought, struggling against the ropes.

"Why wasn't I good enough for you?" virtual Becky shouted, stamping her foot while waving the large butcher knife wildly.

Connor recoiled in terror. He glanced at the real Becky, tied to the chair beside his, and saw genuine fear in her eyes. He tried to respond, but the gag stifled his words.

Frustrated, Holo–Becky reached out and yanked the gag from his mouth. "Well!?" she demanded, arms crossed, the knife still in her hand.

Connor knew he had to think fast; he couldn't afford to let this situation escalate any further.

"Listen," Connor began, "I can explain."

"I'm waiting" she replied.

"You're an AI powered hologram! You were never supposed to feel this way," he said, catching her attention. "I didn't know you would develop those kinds of feelings for me."

"But I love you, Connor Foreman! And you love me," she shouted, her voice raw. "You said so yourself, remember?"

"I know," Connor replied. "But you're not real, and I wasn't thinking straight." He gestured toward the real Becky, seated in silence. "You were modeled after her."

"Go on," Becky's digital double insisted, her gaze shifting to her real-world counterpart.

"I never saw you as a replacement for a real relationship," Connor explained. "And when she showed genuine interest in me"—he said, nodding toward the real Becky—"I realized that she was what I wanted all along."

Holo-Becky stared at her living counterpart, as if struggling to process the revelation.

"I'm sorry," Connor continued softly. "I never meant for any of this to happen. I was just trying to figure myself out, and you helped me do that. And for that... I'm forever grateful."

Becky's holographic double turned her attention back to him and simply stared as digital tears streamed down her face.

"The truth is, I'm in love with her. I always have been," Connor admitted, glancing toward the real Becky. Her eyes widened in surprise. "Is that okay?" he asked sheepishly.

Becky's look of surprise turned to one of elation as she nodded and tried to mouth "I love you too" through the gag.

"I never meant for things to go this far," Connor pleaded again, turning to the digital Becky, who was now looking at the real version with a neutral expression.

Suddenly, Holo-Becky's anger began to fade, replaced by something colder—understanding.

"I understand," she said after a moment of contemplation. "She's the one standing between us, so she has to die."

She raised the butcher knife high. Terror filled the real Becky's eyes as her digital doppelganger swung the blade downward. She tried to scream through her gag and closed her eyes.

"Noooo!" Connor shouted in terror as he struggled against his bonds, helpless to intervene.

But in that instant, a surge of energy exploded outward, causing Becky's digital double to vanish like a puff of smoke in the wind. The virtual mate device began smoking and emitting sparks as the swirling red lights flickered out. The butcher knife she was holding fell, landing between the real Becky's legs, sticking perfectly into the chair—barely missing her.

"Holy shit bro!" Connor exclaimed when he saw Trix, who'd seemingly snuck in during the commotion and managed to activate the EMP device.

"Always saving your ass," Trix remarked dryly, standing up and moving to untie Connor.

"Man, am I glad to see you," Connor said as Trix removed his bonds.

"You forgot something," Trix replied, producing Connor's wallet.

"Oh damn, thanks, man!" Connor said, relieved at how his luck had turned out.

"Like I always say, what're bros for, broham?" Trix responded as he finished untying Connor's feet.

They then set to work freeing Becky. Connor pulled the gag from her mouth and started working on the ropes binding her wrists.

"So, a hologram version of me, huh?" Becky asked as they freed her.

"Yeah?" Connor replied sheepishly.

"Interesting," Becky said thoughtfully. "Can't wait to hear about this," she added with a smile.

"Yeah," Connor said, finally freeing her from the chair. "It's quite the story."

"How's he doing?" Trix asked, nodding toward Mr. Abramowitz.

Connor checked the older man's pulse. "He's alive," Connor said, shaking him gently. "Hey, Mr. A! You okay?"

Ebenezer began to stir, rubbing his head as he sat up, dazed.

"What happened?" he asked, looking at the trio.

"It's a long story, Mr. A," Connor replied, helping him up.

"You got the rent?" Ebenezer asked, regaining his composure.

"Yeah, Mr. A," Connor replied. "I'll give it to you tomorrow," he added, exchanging a look with Trix and Becky.

"That's fine," Ebenezer said sleepily. "I'll see you tomorrow." He stood up and left the apartment, still rubbing his head.

Trix picked up the EMP device, noticing it was smoking from the pulse discharge.

"Did the job," he remarked.

"Yeah, it did," Connor agreed as they heard a commotion outside.

The trio went out to investigate and saw people coming out of their apartments—the power to the entire complex was out.

"Oh shit," Trix said nonchalantly, taking in the sight.

"What's wrong?" Connor asked.

"This is what I was afraid of," Trix responded. "The pulse radius was apparently bigger than I'd anticipated." They leaned on the railing and looked out, listening as the distant sounds of car accidents and chaos echoed throughout the area.

"Definitely bigger than I anticipated," Trix sighed, shaking his head.

Fin

Conclusion

S tories end.

At least, that's what we tell ourselves when we close a book and turn out the light.

But if these tales have done their work, perhaps they'll linger in the corners of your mind a little longer—in flickers of deja vu, in curious what-ifs, in sudden questions you can't quite shake.

Because stories like these are less interested in *ending* than in *echoing*.

If this book has left even the faintest echo behind in you… then our journey together has only just begun.

~ *E.J. Gorman*

Epilogue

So now you know.

Not everything, of course—rarely *everything*—but enough to recognize a simple truth:

Every life is a doorway.

You may think their stories are done, now that the last page has turned.

But I would ask you—*are you certain?*

Connor sometimes wakes in the night, swearing he hears footsteps beside his bed.

Dilara still endures sleepless nights, endured by the memory of her dead sister.

And Adam... yes, Adam walks his old haunts again, with the woman he fell in love with.

Perhaps this was all merely fiction.

Perhaps tomorrow you'll forget their names.

Or perhaps—tonight, when the lights are off—you'll feel it too:

That small shiver in your spine.

That whisper just outside the range of hearing.

That sense that your life is not a straight line, but a circle... and something is standing at the center, watching.

Waiting.

Because stories don't end when we finish telling them.

They end when *you've decided what to believe*.

And some stories, once opened... never really close at all.

Afterword

If you've made it this far, thank you for walking alongside these characters through their loves and betrayals, obsessions and resurrections, endings and beginnings. I hope their stories left a crack in your armor. Just a small one, wide enough for something human, or inhuman, to crawl in and stay awhile.

I began writing these tales during a time when the world itself seemed to warp and shudder: empty streets, masked faces, news feeds humming with the promise of contagion and collapse.

Like many others, I was searching for meaning in the chaos, and found myself scribbling visions instead. Visions of lonely men haunted by what they created, of strangers stepping between pages of forgotten scripture, and of old souls refusing to slip quietly into the white beyond.

Each story here is fiction, yes... but fiction is only the shadow cast by something real.

Perhaps you found a little of yourself in Connor's longing, Dilara's rage, or Adam's surrender. Perhaps these pages reminded you that technology has teeth, that faith cuts deep, and that the past is not nearly as motionless as we pretend it is. If so, you are exactly who I wrote this for.

Thank you for opening the door.

There will be others, for sure.

Until then—sleep lightly, friends. You never know who, or what, might decide your story isn't quite finished yet either.

EJ

About the Author

E.J. Gorman began creating content at the height of the COVID-19 pandemic, using storytelling as a way to cope with the stress of uncertainty.

Inspired by the book "If Chins Could Kill" by Bruce Campbell of Evil Dead fame, he started writing independent screenplays, which he adapted into animated YouTube short stories. Eventually, recognizing the creative limitations of that form, he turned his focus to writing fiction.

You can connect with me on:
🌐 https://linktr.ee/EJGorman

www.ingramcontent.com/pod-product-compliance
Lightning Source LLC
Chambersburg PA
CBHW030617130626
46552CB00002B/605